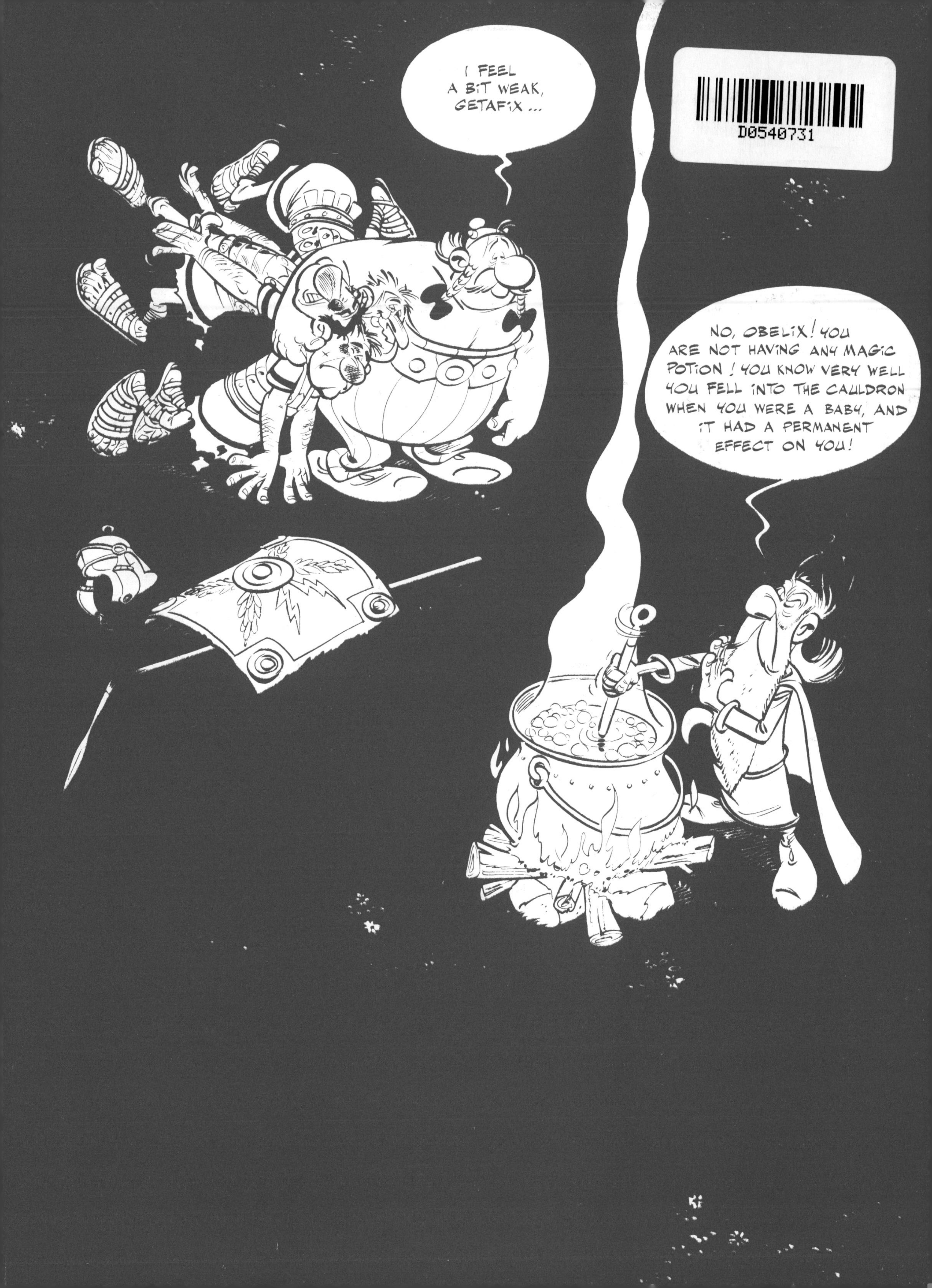

I FEEL A BIT WEAK, GETAFIX ...
NO, OBELIX! YOU ARE NOT HAVING ANY MAGIC POTION! YOU KNOW VERY WELL YOU FELL INTO THE CAULDRON WHEN YOU WERE A BABY, AND IT HAD A PERMANENT EFFECT ON YOU!

D0540731

GOSCINNY AND UDERZO
PRESENT
An Asterix Adventure

ASTERIX
AND THE
GOTHS

Written by RENÉ GOSCINNY *and Illustrated by* ALBERT UDERZO

Translated by Anthea Bell *and* Derek Hockridge

© 1963 GOSCINNY/UDERZO

Revised edition and English translation © 2004 HACHETTE
Original title: *Astérix et les Goths*

Exclusive licensee: Orion Publishing Group
Translators: Anthea Bell and Derek Hockridge
Typography: Bryony Newhouse

This revised edition first published in Great Britain by Orion Publishing Group

This paperback edition first published in 2004 by Orion Books Ltd,
Orion House, 5 Upper Saint Martin's Lane, London WC2H 9EA

5 7 9 10 8 6

Printed in France by Partenaires

http://gb.asterix.com
www.orionbooks.co.uk

A CIP record for this book is available from the British Library

ISBN 0 75286 614 1 (cased)
ISBN 0 75286 615 X (paperback)

Distributed in the United States of America by Sterling Publishing Co. Inc.
387 Park Avenue South, New York, NY 10016

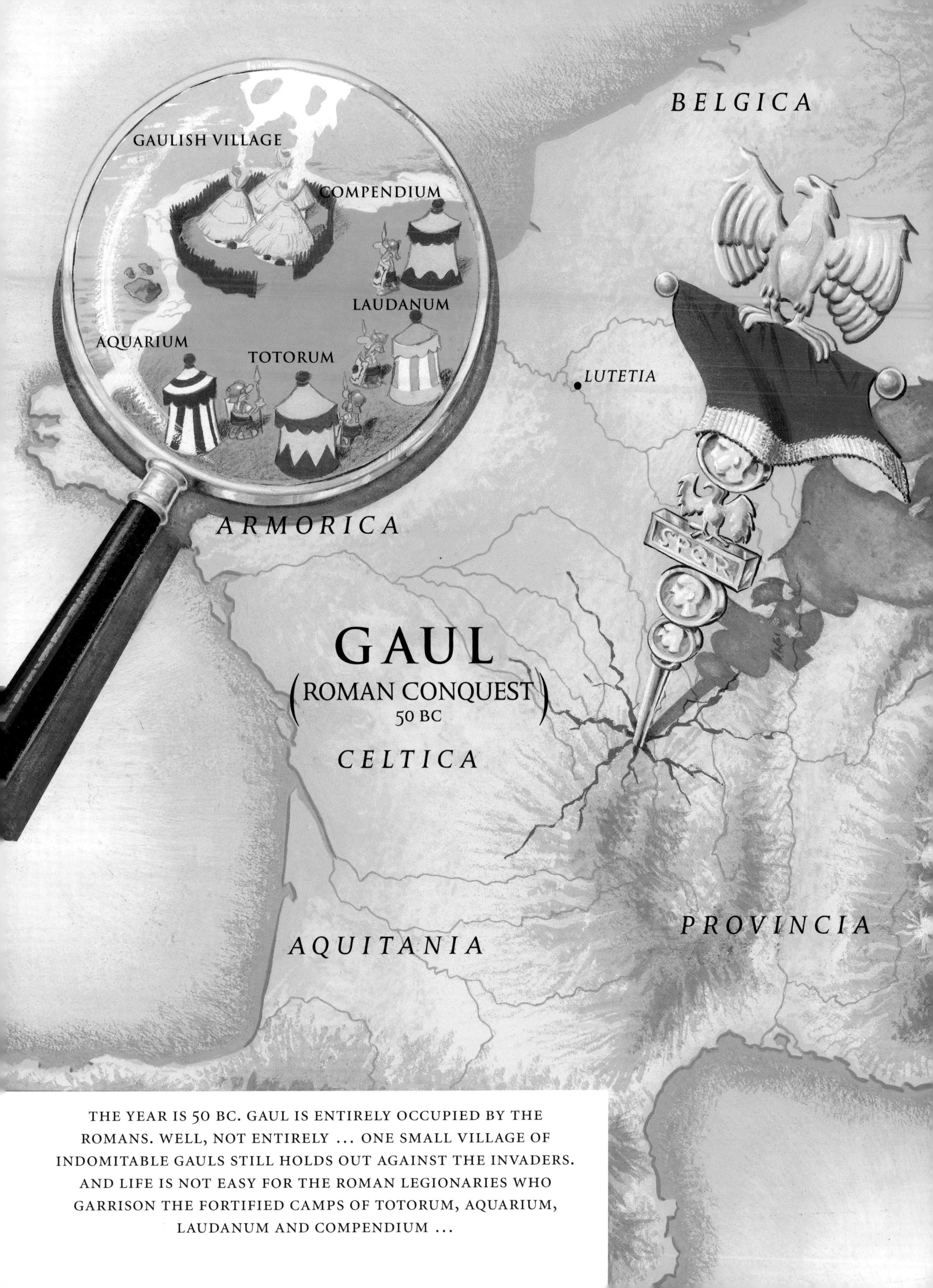
BELGICA
GAULISH VILLAGE
COMPENDIUM
LAUDANUM
AQUARIUM
TOTORUM
LUTETIA
SPQR
ARMORICA
GAUL
(ROMAN CONQUEST 50 BC)
CELTICA
PROVINCIA
AQUITANIA

THE YEAR IS 50 BC. GAUL IS ENTIRELY OCCUPIED BY THE ROMANS. WELL, NOT ENTIRELY ... ONE SMALL VILLAGE OF INDOMITABLE GAULS STILL HOLDS OUT AGAINST THE INVADERS. AND LIFE IS NOT EASY FOR THE ROMAN LEGIONARIES WHO GARRISON THE FORTIFIED CAMPS OF TOTORUM, AQUARIUM, LAUDANUM AND COMPENDIUM ...

ASTERIX, THE HERO OF THESE ADVENTURES. A SHREWD, CUNNING LITTLE WARRIOR, ALL PERILOUS MISSIONS ARE IMMEDIATELY ENTRUSTED TO HIM. ASTERIX GETS HIS SUPERHUMAN STRENGTH FROM THE MAGIC POTION BREWED BY THE DRUID GETAFIX . . .

OBELIX, ASTERIX'S INSEPARABLE FRIEND. A MENHIR DELIVERY MAN BY TRADE, ADDICTED TO WILD BOAR. OBELIX IS ALWAYS READY TO DROP EVERYTHING AND GO OFF ON A NEW ADVENTURE WITH ASTERIX – SO LONG AS THERE'S WILD BOAR TO EAT, AND PLENTY OF FIGHTING. HIS CONSTANT COMPANION IS DOGMATIX, THE ONLY KNOWN CANINE ECOLOGIST, WHO HOWLS WITH DESPAIR WHEN A TREE IS CUT DOWN.

GETAFIX, THE VENERABLE VILLAGE DRUID, GATHERS MISTLETOE AND BREWS MAGIC POTIONS. HIS SPECIALITY IS THE POTION WHICH GIVES THE DRINKER SUPERHUMAN STRENGTH. BUT GETAFIX ALSO HAS OTHER RECIPES UP HIS SLEEVE . . .

CACOFONIX, THE BARD. OPINION IS DIVIDED AS TO HIS MUSICAL GIFTS. CACOFONIX THINKS HE'S A GENIUS. EVERY-ONE ELSE THINKS HE'S UNSPEAKABLE. BUT SO LONG AS HE DOESN'T SPEAK, LET ALONE SING, EVERYBODY LIKES HIM . . .

FINALLY, VITALSTATISTIX, THE CHIEF OF THE TRIBE. MAJESTIC, BRAVE AND HOT-TEMPERED, THE OLD WARRIOR IS RESPECTED BY HIS MEN AND FEARED BY HIS ENEMIES. VITALSTATISTIX HIMSELF HAS ONLY ONE FEAR, HE IS AFRAID THE SKY MAY FALL ON HIS HEAD TOMORROW. BUT AS HE ALWAYS SAYS, TOMORROW NEVER COMES.

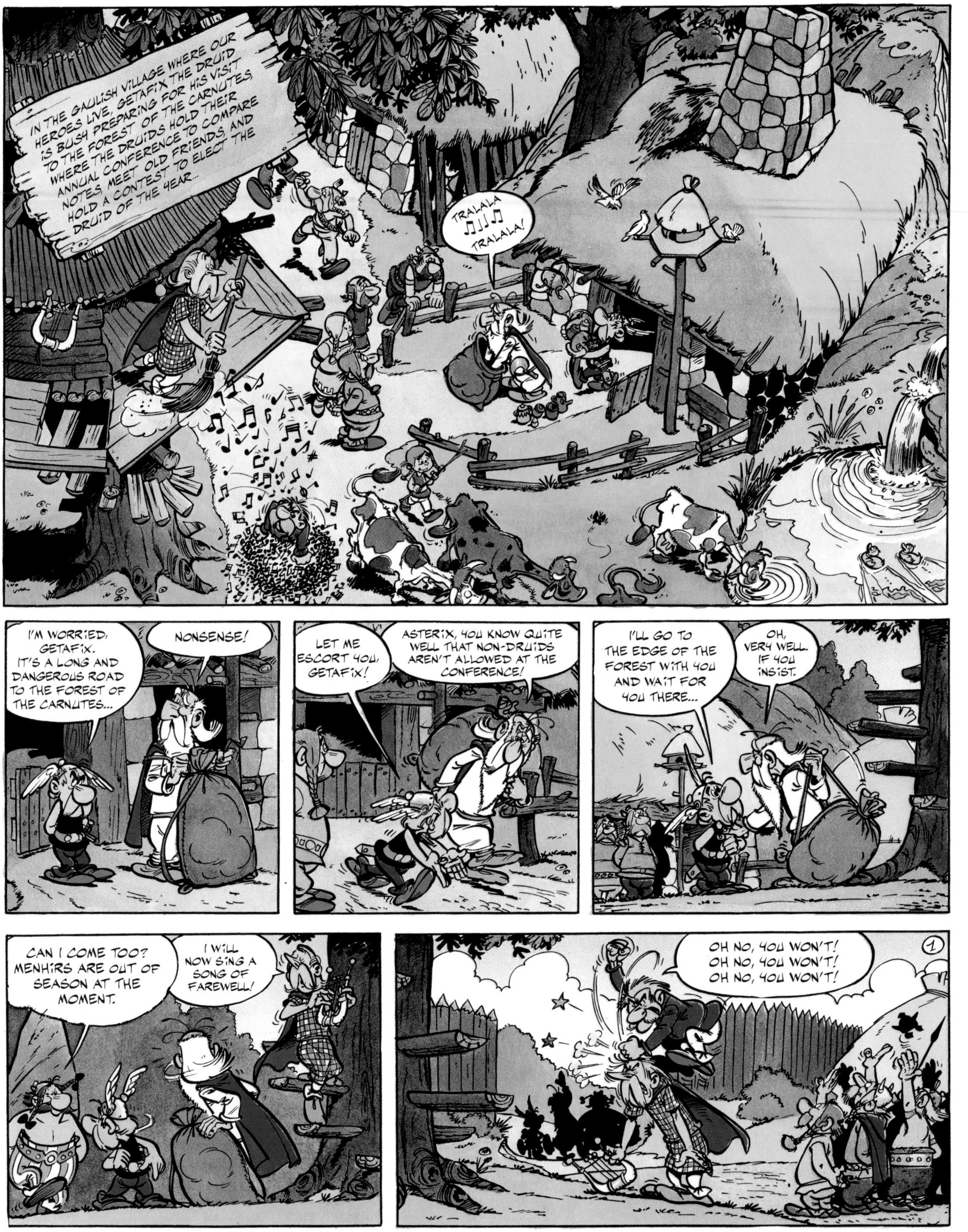
IN THE GAULISH VILLAGE WHERE OUR HEROES LIVE, GETAFIX THE DRUID IS BUSY PREPARING FOR HIS VISIT TO THE FOREST OF THE CARNUTES, WHERE THE DRUIDS HOLD THEIR ANNUAL CONFERENCE TO COMPARE NOTES, MEET OLD FRIENDS, AND HOLD A CONTEST TO ELECT THE DRUID OF THE YEAR...
TRALALA ♫♩♩♫ TRALALA!
I'M WORRIED, GETAFIX. IT'S A LONG AND DANGEROUS ROAD TO THE FOREST OF THE CARNUTES...
NONSENSE!
LET ME ESCORT YOU, GETAFIX!
ASTERIX, YOU KNOW QUITE WELL THAT NON-DRUIDS AREN'T ALLOWED AT THE CONFERENCE!
I'LL GO TO THE EDGE OF THE FOREST WITH YOU AND WAIT FOR YOU THERE...
OH, VERY WELL. IF YOU INSIST.
CAN I COME TOO? MENHIRS ARE OUT OF SEASON AT THE MOMENT.
I WILL NOW SING A SONG OF FAREWELL!
OH NO, YOU WON'T! OH NO, YOU WON'T! OH NO, YOU WON'T!
1

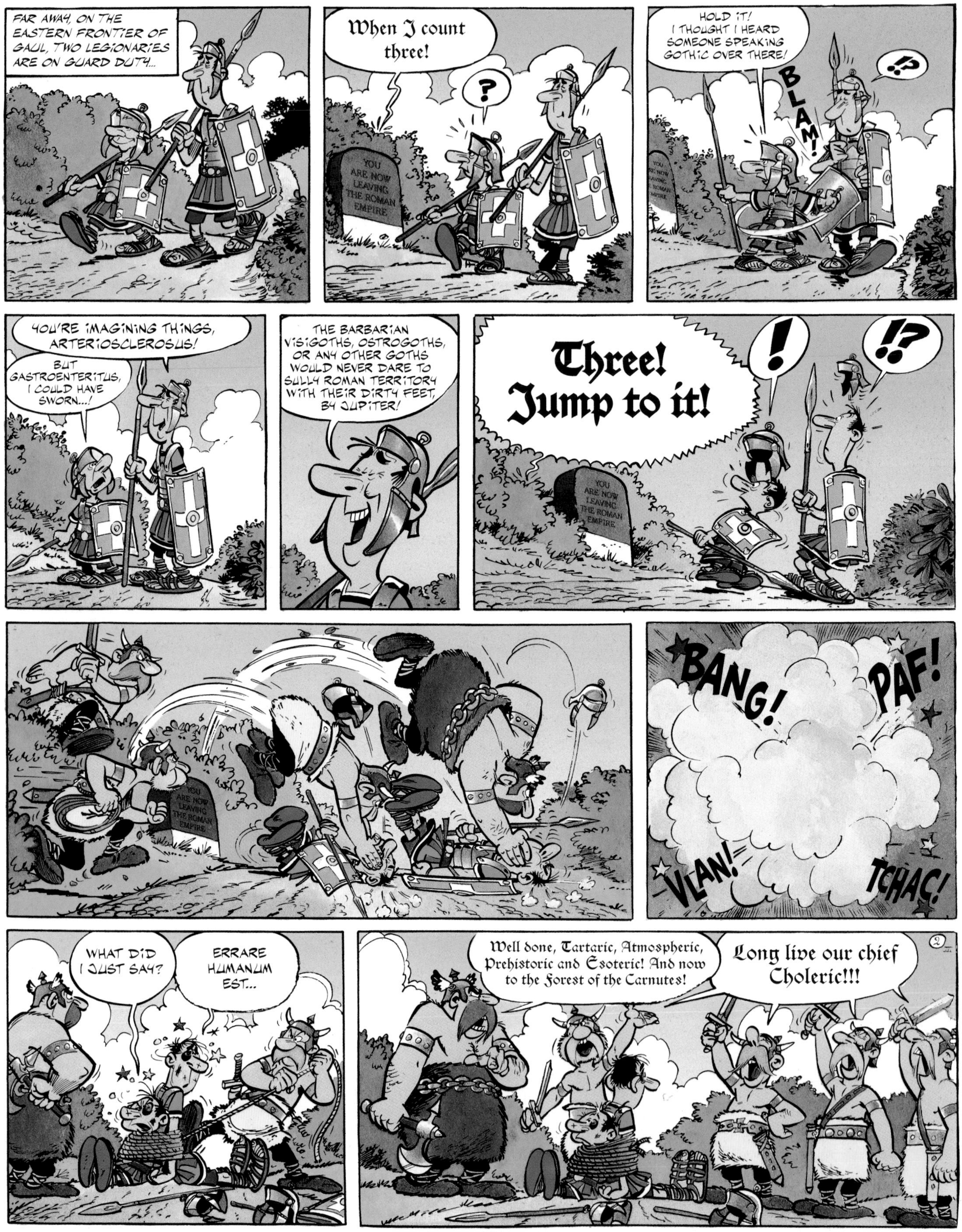
FAR AWAY, ON THE EASTERN FRONTIER OF GAUL, TWO LEGIONARIES ARE ON GUARD DUTY...
When I count three!
?
YOU ARE NOW LEAVING THE ROMAN EMPIRE
HOLD IT! I THOUGHT I HEARD SOMEONE SPEAKING GOTHIC OVER THERE!
BLAM!
!?
YOU'RE IMAGINING THINGS, ARTERIOSCLEROSUS!
BUT GASTROENTERITUS, I COULD HAVE SWORN...!
THE BARBARIAN VISIGOTHS, OSTROGOTHS, OR ANY OTHER GOTHS WOULD NEVER DARE TO SULLY ROMAN TERRITORY WITH THEIR DIRTY FEET, BY JUPITER!
Three! Jump to it!
!
!?
YOU ARE NOW LEAVING THE ROMAN EMPIRE
YOU ARE NOW LEAVING THE ROMAN EMPIRE
BANG!
PAF!
VLAN!
TCHAC!
WHAT DID I JUST SAY?
ERRARE HUMANUM EST...
Well done, Tartaric, Atmospheric, Prehistoric and Esoteric! And now to the Forest of the Carnutes!
Long live our chief Choleric!!!

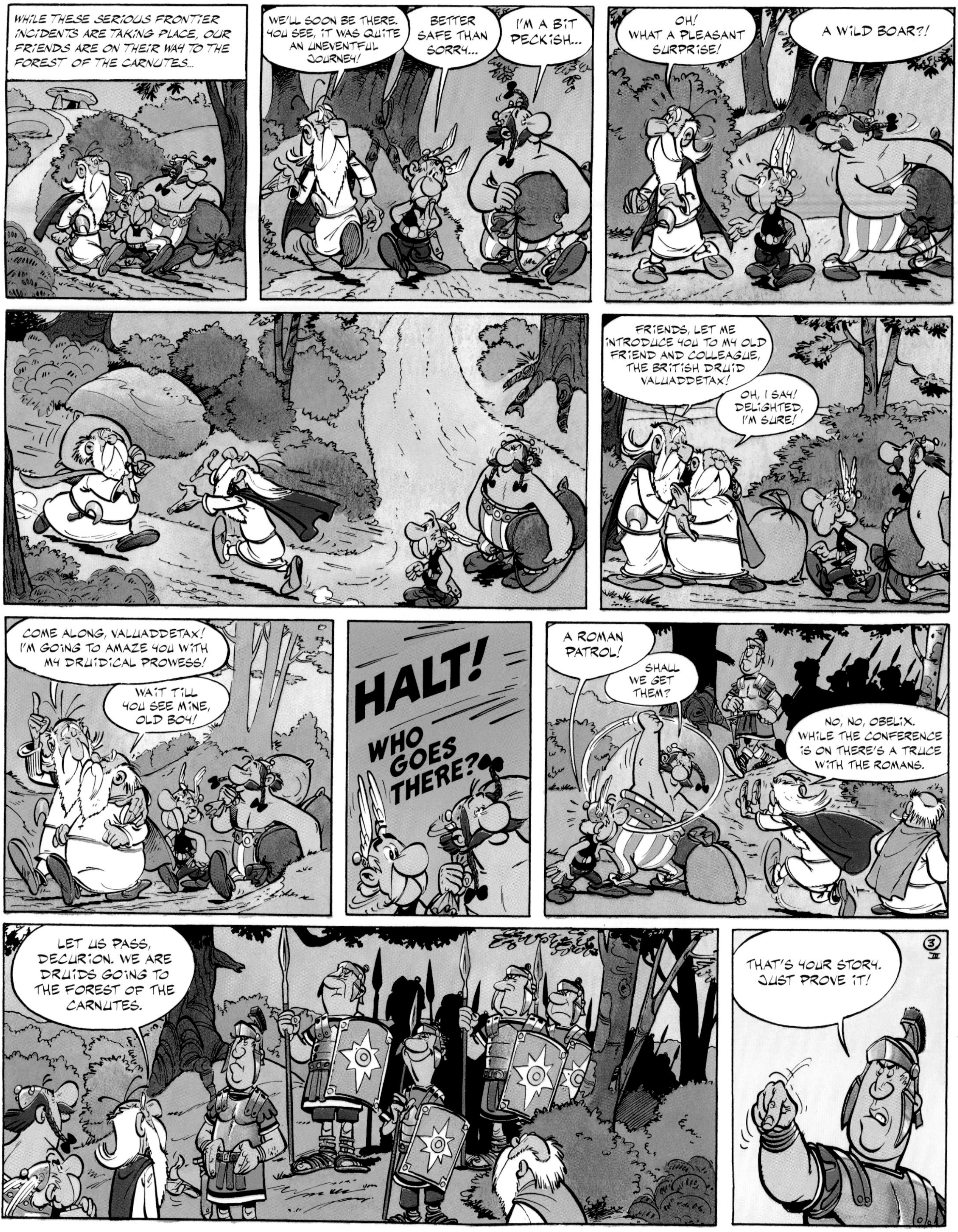

WHILE THESE SERIOUS FRONTIER INCIDENTS ARE TAKING PLACE, OUR FRIENDS ARE ON THEIR WAY TO THE FOREST OF THE CARNUTES...
WE'LL SOON BE THERE. YOU SEE, IT WAS QUITE AN UNEVENTFUL JOURNEY!
BETTER SAFE THAN SORRY...
I'M A BIT PECKISH...
OH! WHAT A PLEASANT SURPRISE!
A WILD BOAR?!
FRIENDS, LET ME INTRODUCE YOU TO MY OLD FRIEND AND COLLEAGUE, THE BRITISH DRUID VALUADDETAX!
OH, I SAY! DELIGHTED, I'M SURE!
COME ALONG, VALUADDETAX! I'M GOING TO AMAZE YOU WITH MY DRUIDICAL PROWESS!
WAIT TILL YOU SEE MINE, OLD BOY!
HALT!
WHO GOES THERE?
A ROMAN PATROL!
SHALL WE GET THEM?
NO, NO, OBELIX. WHILE THE CONFERENCE IS ON THERE'S A TRUCE WITH THE ROMANS.
LET US PASS, DECURION. WE ARE DRUIDS GOING TO THE FOREST OF THE CARNUTES.
THAT'S YOUR STORY. JUST PROVE IT!

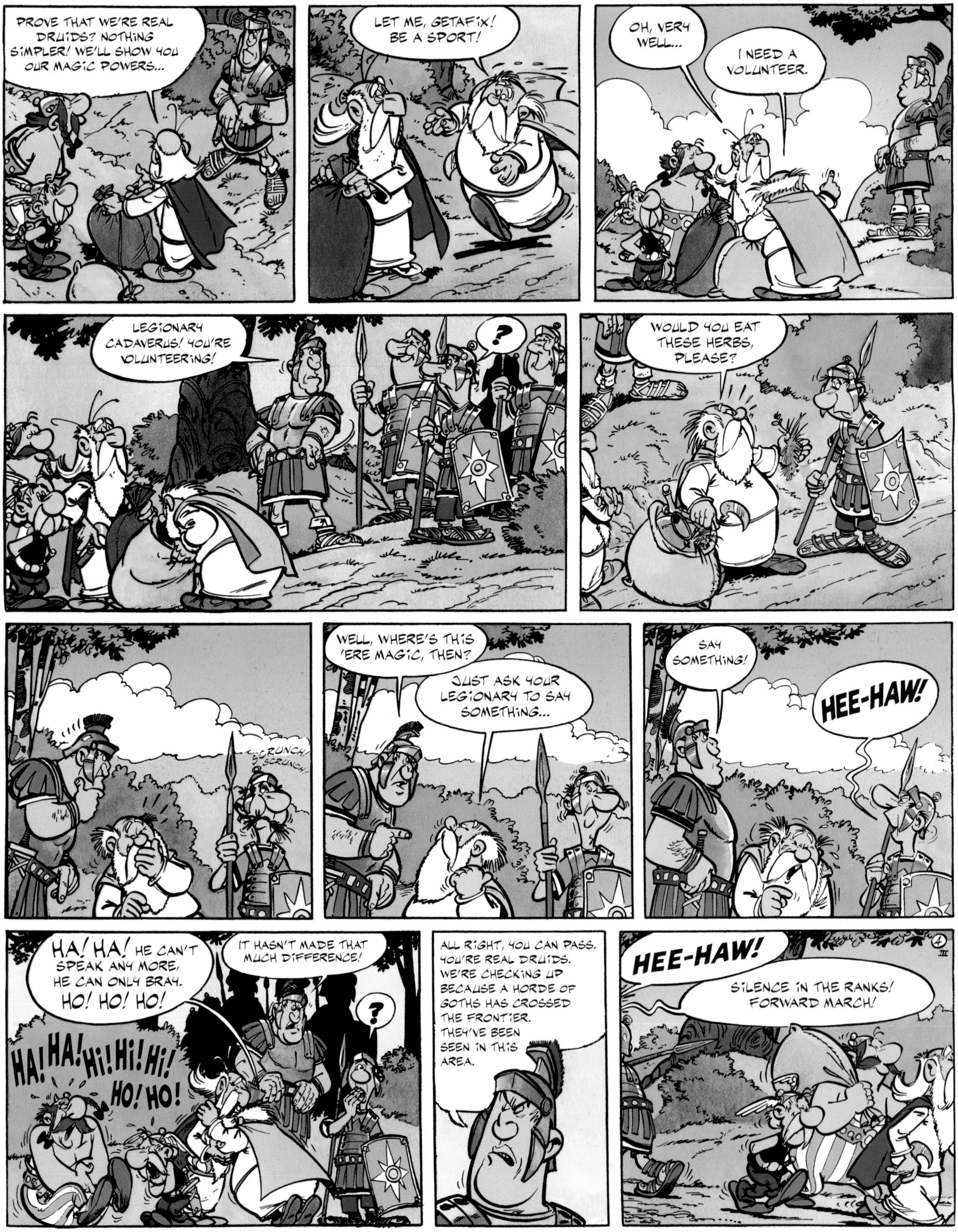
PROVE THAT WE'RE REAL DRUIDS? NOTHING SIMPLER! WE'LL SHOW YOU OUR MAGIC POWERS...
LET ME, GETAFIX! BE A SPORT!
OH, VERY WELL...
I NEED A VOLUNTEER.
LEGIONARY CADAVERUS! YOU'RE VOLUNTEERING!
?
WOULD YOU EAT THESE HERBS, PLEASE?
CRUNCH! SCRUNCH!
WELL, WHERE'S THIS 'ERE MAGIC, THEN?
JUST ASK YOUR LEGIONARY TO SAY SOMETHING...
SAY SOMETHING!
HEE-HAW!
HA! HA! HE CAN'T SPEAK ANY MORE, HE CAN ONLY BRAY. HO! HO! HO!
IT HASN'T MADE THAT MUCH DIFFERENCE!
HA! HA! HI! HI! HI! HO! HO!
?
ALL RIGHT, YOU CAN PASS. YOU'RE REAL DRUIDS. WE'RE CHECKING UP BECAUSE A HORDE OF GOTHS HAS CROSSED THE FRONTIER. THEY'VE BEEN SEEN IN THIS AREA.
HEE-HAW!
SILENCE IN THE RANKS! FORWARD MARCH!

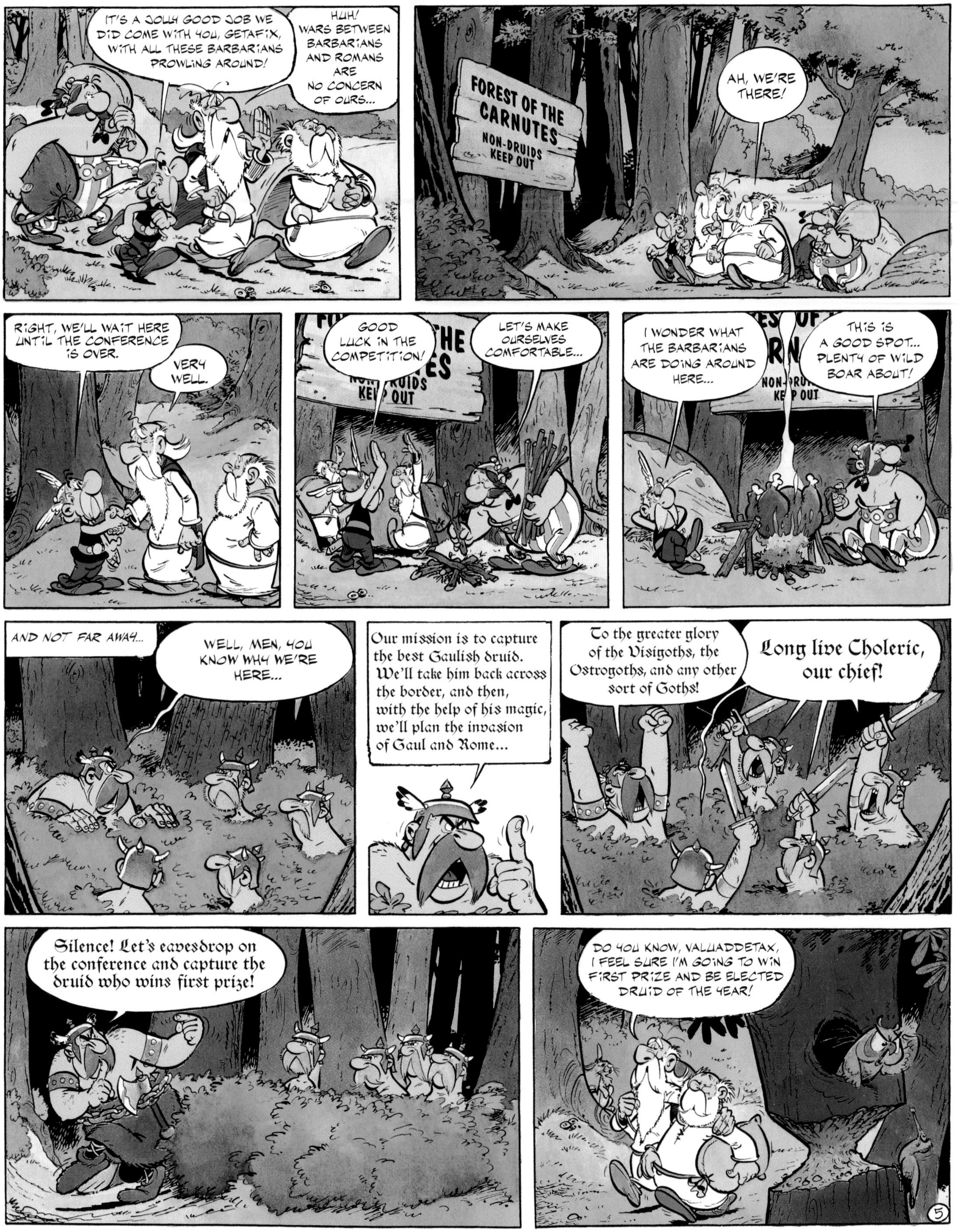
IT'S A JOLLY GOOD JOB WE DID COME WITH YOU, GETAFIX, WITH ALL THESE BARBARIANS PROWLING AROUND!
HUH! WARS BETWEEN BARBARIANS AND ROMANS ARE NO CONCERN OF OURS...
FOREST OF THE CARNUTES
NON-DRUIDS KEEP OUT
AH, WE'RE THERE!
RIGHT, WE'LL WAIT HERE UNTIL THE CONFERENCE IS OVER.
VERY WELL.
GOOD LUCK IN THE COMPETITION!
LET'S MAKE OURSELVES COMFORTABLE...
I WONDER WHAT THE BARBARIANS ARE DOING AROUND HERE...
THIS IS A GOOD SPOT... PLENTY OF WILD BOAR ABOUT!
AND NOT FAR AWAY...
WELL, MEN, YOU KNOW WHY WE'RE HERE...
Our mission is to capture the best Gaulish druid. We'll take him back across the border, and then, with the help of his magic, we'll plan the invasion of Gaul and Rome...
To the greater glory of the Visigoths, the Ostrogoths, and any other sort of Goths!
Long live Choleric, our chief!
Silence! Let's eavesdrop on the conference and capture the druid who wins first prize!
DO YOU KNOW, VALUADDETAX, I FEEL SURE I'M GOING TO WIN FIRST PRIZE AND BE ELECTED DRUID OF THE YEAR!
5

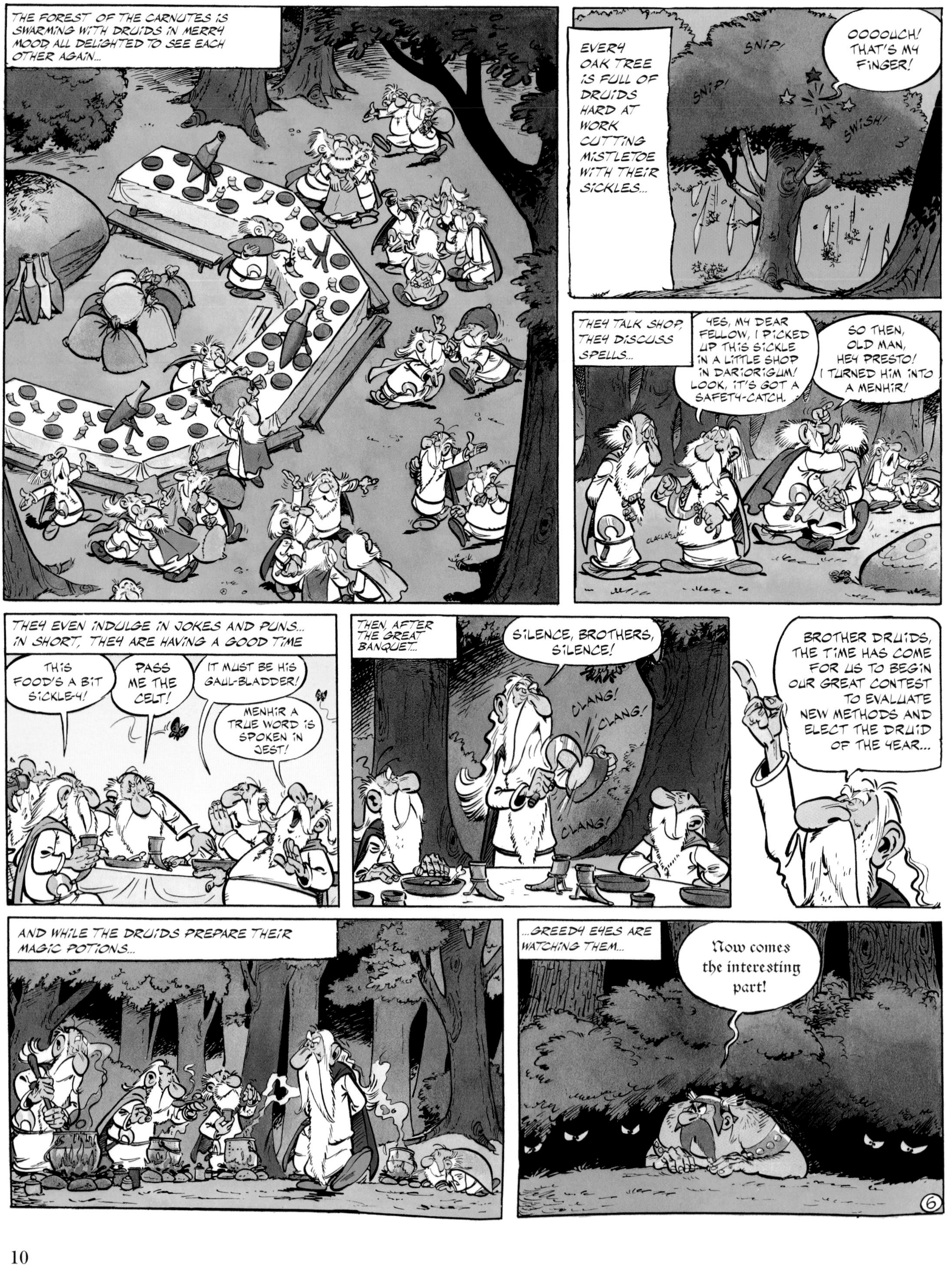
THE FOREST OF THE CARNUTES IS SWARMING WITH DRUIDS IN MERRY MOOD ALL DELIGHTED TO SEE EACH OTHER AGAIN...
EVERY OAK TREE IS FULL OF DRUIDS HARD AT WORK CUTTING MISTLETOE WITH THEIR SICKLES...
SNIP!
SNIP!
SWISH!
OOOOUCH! THAT'S MY FINGER!
THEY TALK SHOP, THEY DISCUSS SPELLS...
YES, MY DEAR FELLOW, I PICKED UP THIS SICKLE IN A LITTLE SHOP IN DARIORIGUM! LOOK, IT'S GOT A SAFETY-CATCH.
SO THEN, OLD MAN, HEY PRESTO! I TURNED HIM INTO A MENHIR!
THEY EVEN INDULGE IN JOKES AND PUNS... IN SHORT, THEY ARE HAVING A GOOD TIME
THIS FOOD'S A BIT SICKLE-Y!
PASS ME THE CELT!
IT MUST BE HIS GAUL-BLADDER!
MENHIR A TRUE WORD IS SPOKEN IN JEST!
THEN, AFTER THE GREAT BANQUET...
SILENCE, BROTHERS, SILENCE!
CLANG!
CLANG!
CLANG!
BROTHER DRUIDS, THE TIME HAS COME FOR US TO BEGIN OUR GREAT CONTEST TO EVALUATE NEW METHODS AND ELECT THE DRUID OF THE YEAR...
AND WHILE THE DRUIDS PREPARE THEIR MAGIC POTIONS...
...GREEDY EYES ARE WATCHING THEM...
Now comes the interesting part!

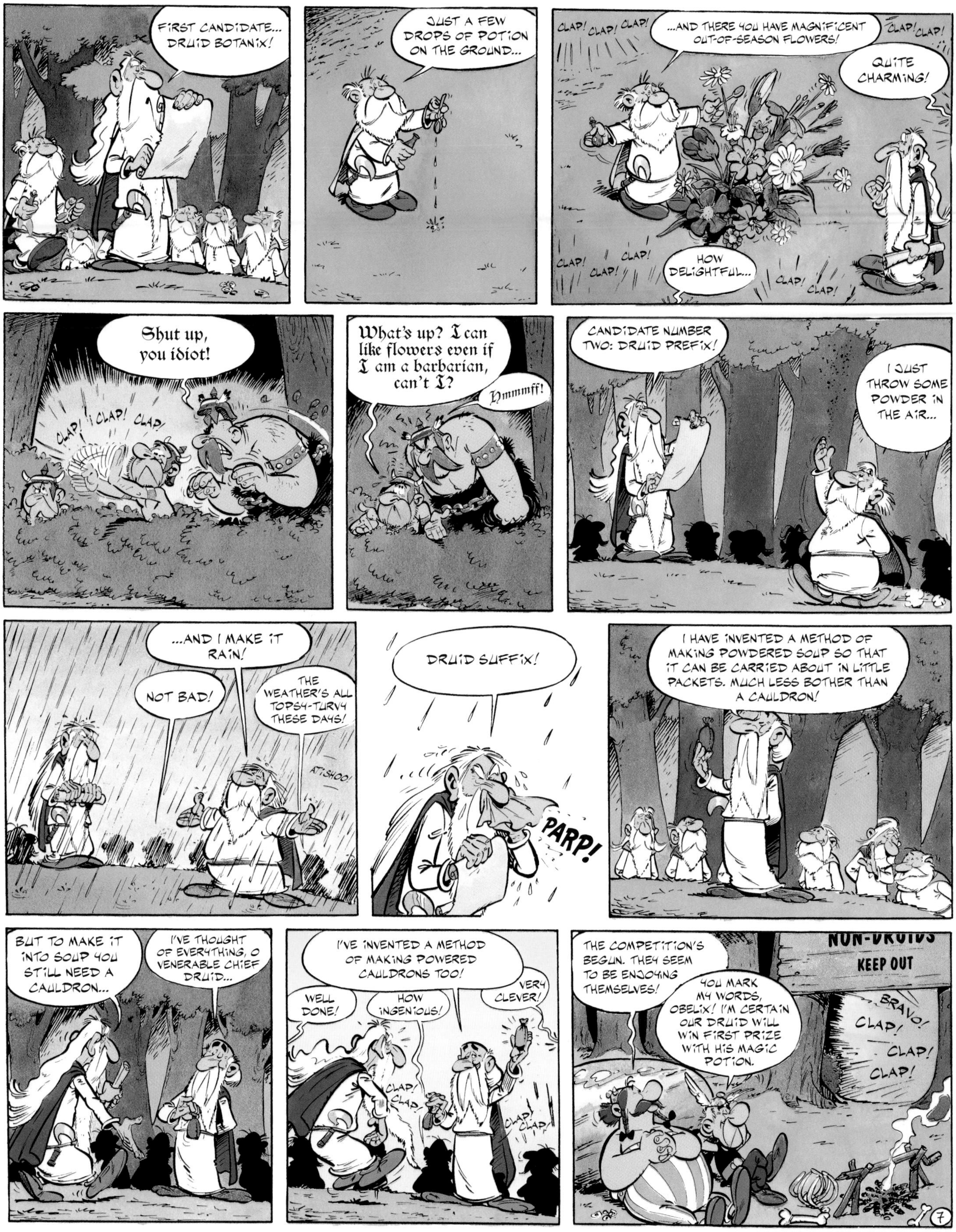

FIRST CANDIDATE... DRUID BOTANIX!
JUST A FEW DROPS OF POTION ON THE GROUND...
CLAP! CLAP! CLAP!
...AND THERE YOU HAVE MAGNIFICENT OUT-OF-SEASON FLOWERS!
CLAP! CLAP!
QUITE CHARMING!
CLAP! CLAP! CLAP!
HOW DELIGHTFUL...
CLAP! CLAP!
Shut up, you idiot!
CLAP! CLAP! CLAP!
What's up? I can like flowers even if I am a barbarian, can't I?
Hmmmff!
CANDIDATE NUMBER TWO: DRUID PREFIX!
I JUST THROW SOME POWDER IN THE AIR...
...AND I MAKE IT RAIN!
NOT BAD!
THE WEATHER'S ALL TOPSY-TURVY THESE DAYS!
ATISHOO!
DRUID SUFFIX!
PARP!
I HAVE INVENTED A METHOD OF MAKING POWDERED SOUP SO THAT IT CAN BE CARRIED ABOUT IN LITTLE PACKETS. MUCH LESS BOTHER THAN A CAULDRON!
BUT TO MAKE IT INTO SOUP YOU STILL NEED A CAULDRON...
I'VE THOUGHT OF EVERYTHING, O VENERABLE CHIEF DRUID...
I'VE INVENTED A METHOD OF MAKING POWERED CAULDRONS TOO!
WELL DONE!
HOW INGENIOUS!
VERY CLEVER!
CLAP! CLAP!
CLAP! CLAP!
NON-DRUIDS KEEP OUT
THE COMPETITION'S BEGUN. THEY SEEM TO BE ENJOYING THEMSELVES!
YOU MARK MY WORDS, OBELIX! I'M CERTAIN OUR DRUID WILL WIN FIRST PRIZE WITH HIS MAGIC POTION.
BRAVO!
CLAP!
CLAP!
CLAP!
7

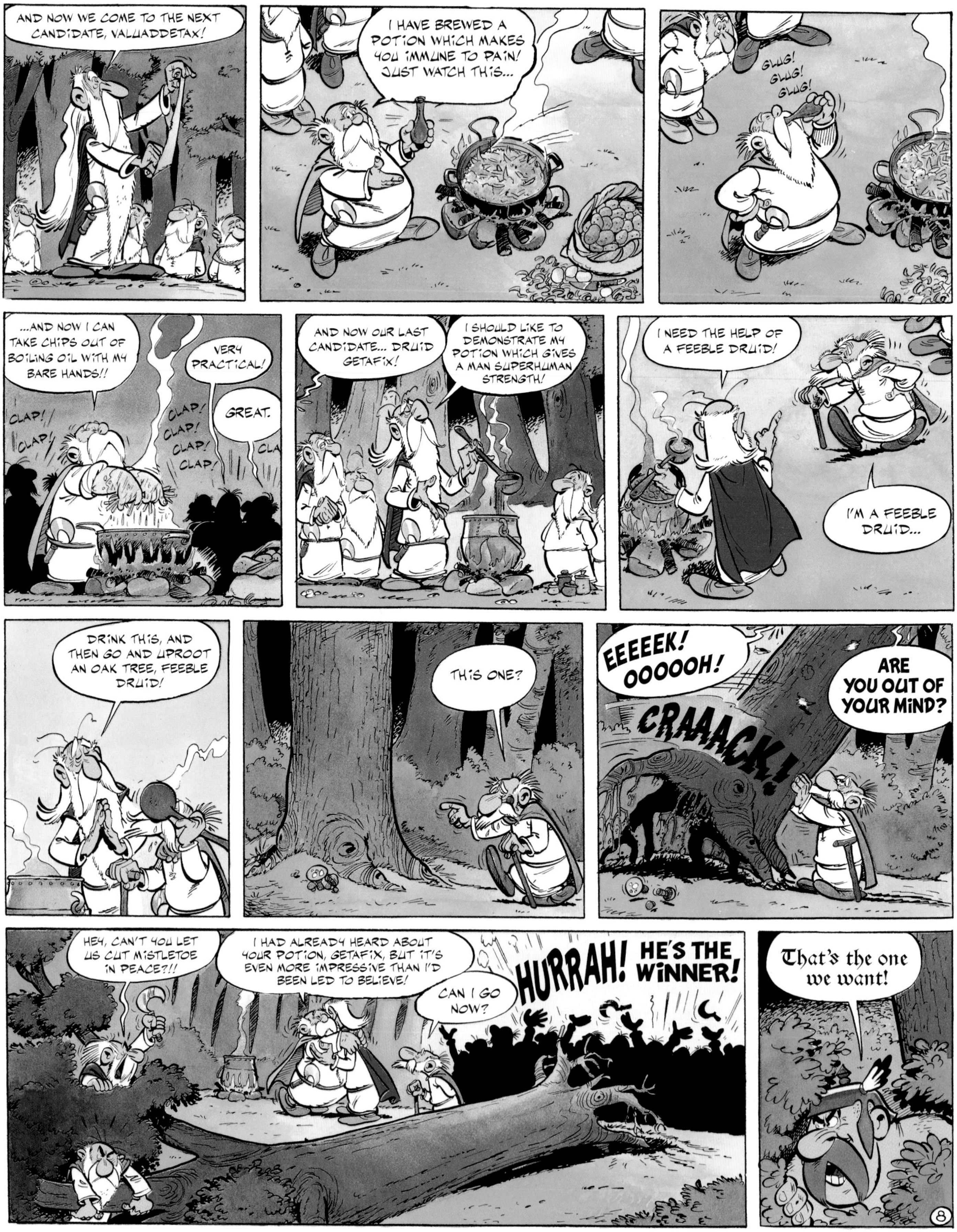

AND NOW WE COME TO THE NEXT CANDIDATE, VALUADDETAX!
I HAVE BREWED A POTION WHICH MAKES YOU IMMUNE TO PAIN! JUST WATCH THIS...
GLUG! GLUG! GLUG!
...AND NOW I CAN TAKE CHIPS OUT OF BOILING OIL WITH MY BARE HANDS!!
CLAP! CLAP!
VERY PRACTICAL!
CLAP! CLAP! CLAP! CLAP!
GREAT.
AND NOW OUR LAST CANDIDATE... DRUID GETAFIX!
I SHOULD LIKE TO DEMONSTRATE MY POTION WHICH GIVES A MAN SUPERHUMAN STRENGTH!
I NEED THE HELP OF A FEEBLE DRUID!
I'M A FEEBLE DRUID...
DRINK THIS, AND THEN GO AND UPROOT AN OAK TREE, FEEBLE DRUID!
THIS ONE?
EEEEEK! OOOOOH!
CRAAACK!
ARE YOU OUT OF YOUR MIND?
HEY, CAN'T YOU LET US CUT MISTLETOE IN PEACE?!!
I HAD ALREADY HEARD ABOUT YOUR POTION, GETAFIX, BUT IT'S EVEN MORE IMPRESSIVE THAN I'D BEEN LED TO BELIEVE!
CAN I GO NOW?
HURRAH! HE'S THE WINNER!
That's the one we want!
8

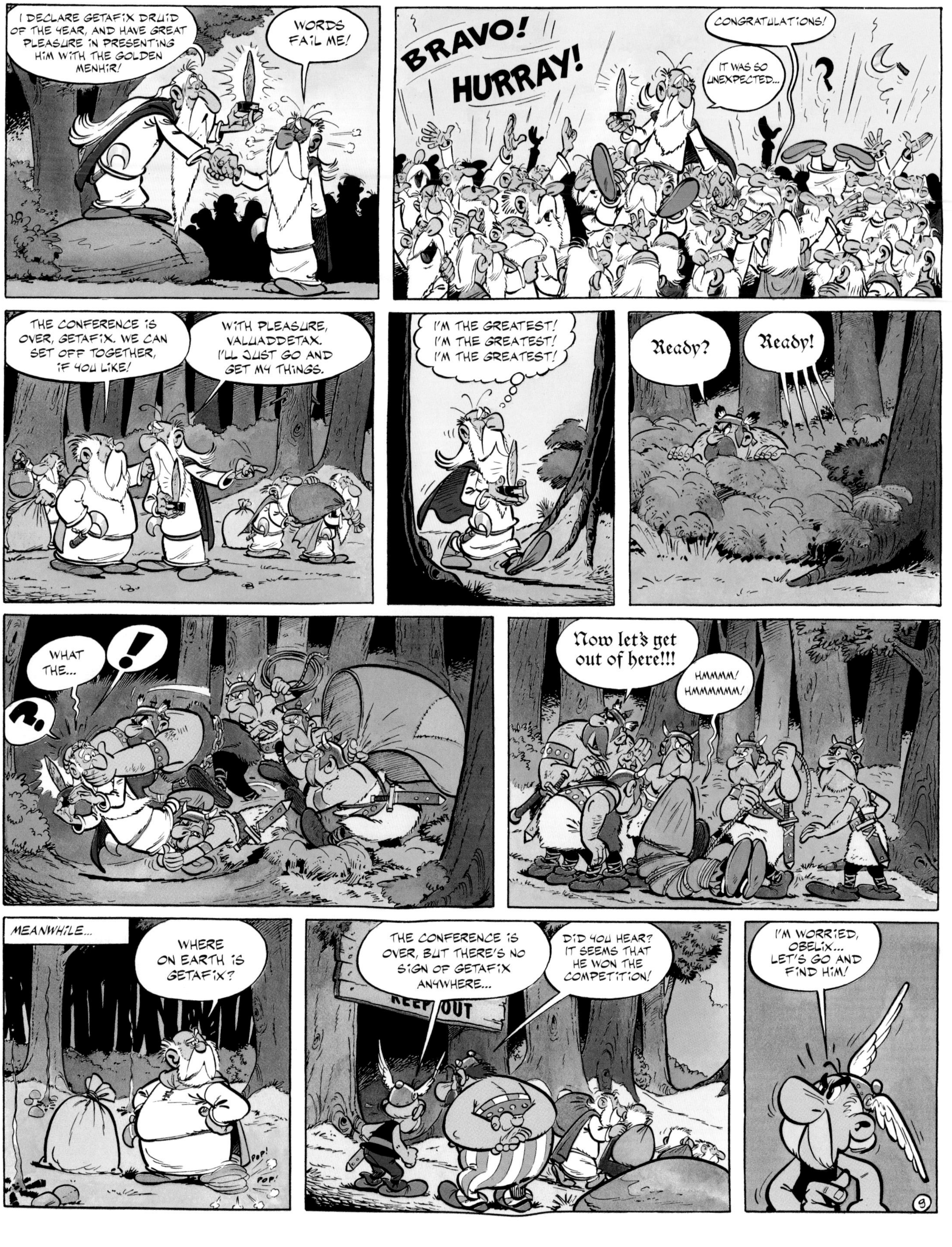
I DECLARE GETAFIX DRUID OF THE YEAR, AND HAVE GREAT PLEASURE IN PRESENTING HIM WITH THE GOLDEN MENHIR!
WORDS FAIL ME!
BRAVO!
HURRAY!
CONGRATULATIONS!
IT WAS SO UNEXPECTED...
THE CONFERENCE IS OVER, GETAFIX. WE CAN SET OFF TOGETHER, IF YOU LIKE!
WITH PLEASURE, VALUADDETAX. I'LL JUST GO AND GET MY THINGS.
I'M THE GREATEST! I'M THE GREATEST! I'M THE GREATEST!
Ready?
Ready!
WHAT THE...
!
Now let's get out of here!!!
HMMMM! HMMMMMM!
MEANWHILE...
WHERE ON EARTH IS GETAFIX?
POP! POP!
THE CONFERENCE IS OVER, BUT THERE'S NO SIGN OF GETAFIX ANYWHERE...
DID YOU HEAR? IT SEEMS THAT HE WON THE COMPETITION!
KEEP OUT
I'M WORRIED, OBELIX... LET'S GO AND FIND HIM!
9

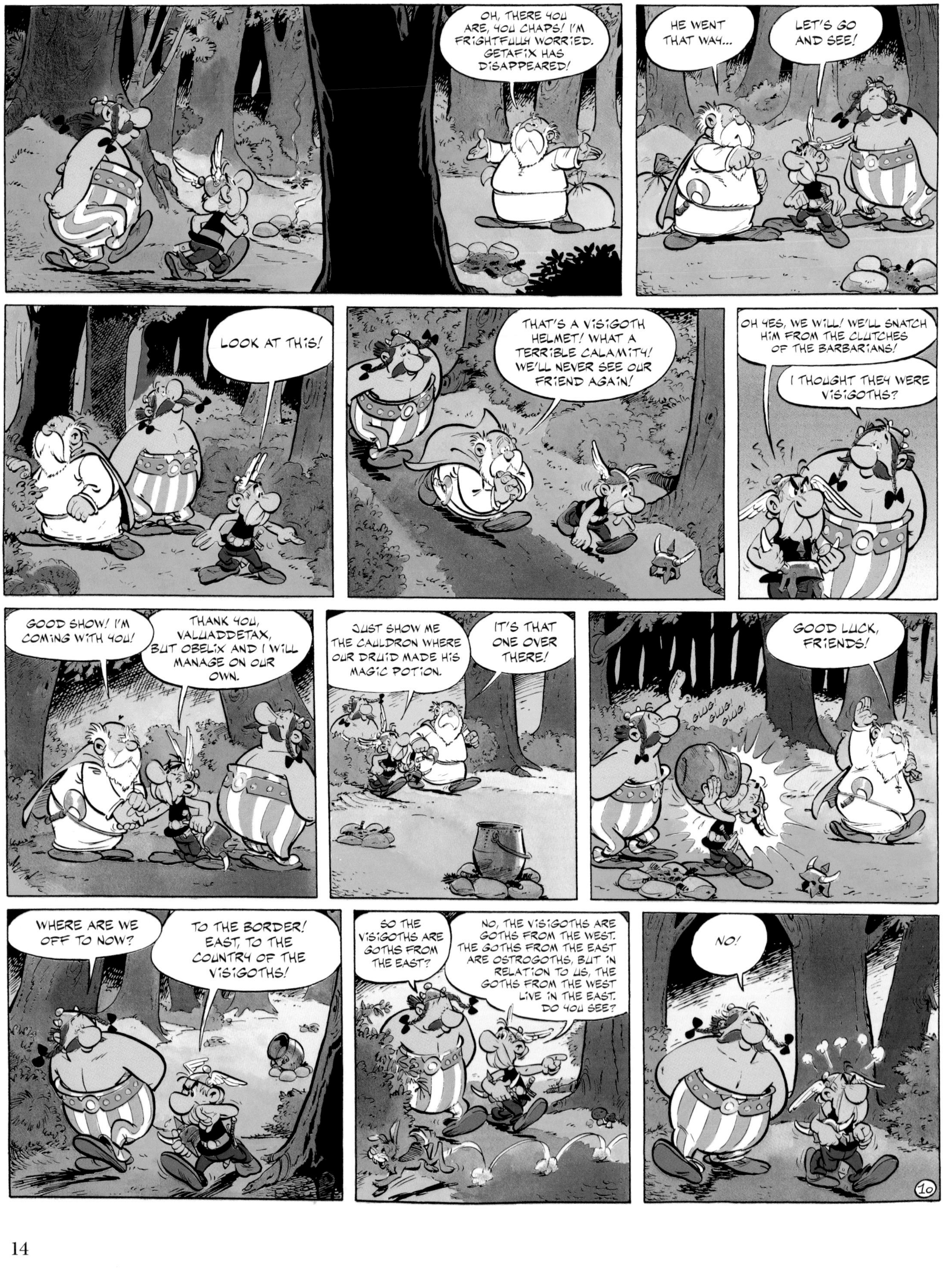

OH, THERE YOU ARE, YOU CHAPS! I'M FRIGHTFULLY WORRIED. GETAFIX HAS DISAPPEARED!
HE WENT THAT WAY...
LET'S GO AND SEE!
LOOK AT THIS!
THAT'S A VISIGOTH HELMET! WHAT A TERRIBLE CALAMITY! WE'LL NEVER SEE OUR FRIEND AGAIN!
OH YES, WE WILL! WE'LL SNATCH HIM FROM THE CLUTCHES OF THE BARBARIANS!
I THOUGHT THEY WERE VISIGOTHS?
GOOD SHOW! I'M COMING WITH YOU!
THANK YOU, VALUADDETAX, BUT OBELIX AND I WILL MANAGE ON OUR OWN.
JUST SHOW ME THE CAULDRON WHERE OUR DRUID MADE HIS MAGIC POTION.
IT'S THAT ONE OVER THERE!
GOOD LUCK, FRIENDS!
GLUG! GLUG! GLUG!
WHERE ARE WE OFF TO NOW?
TO THE BORDER! EAST, TO THE COUNTRY OF THE VISIGOTHS!
SO THE VISIGOTHS ARE GOTHS FROM THE EAST?
NO, THE VISIGOTHS ARE GOTHS FROM THE WEST. THE GOTHS FROM THE EAST ARE OSTROGOTHS, BUT IN RELATION TO US, THE GOTHS FROM THE WEST LIVE IN THE EAST. DO YOU SEE?
NO!
10

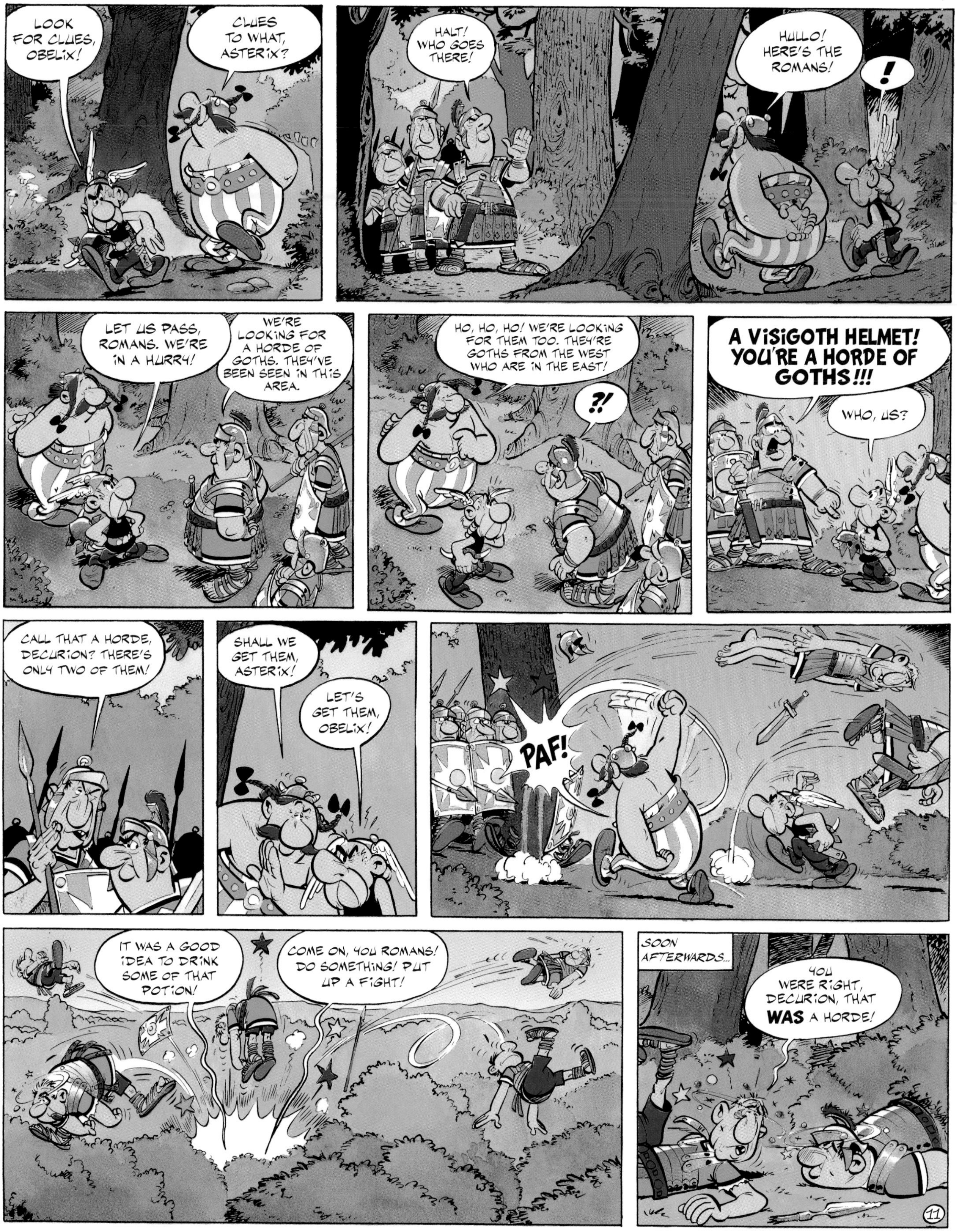
LOOK FOR CLUES, OBELIX!
CLUES TO WHAT, ASTERIX?
HALT! WHO GOES THERE!
HULLO! HERE'S THE ROMANS!
!
LET US PASS, ROMANS. WE'RE IN A HURRY!
WE'RE LOOKING FOR A HORDE OF GOTHS. THEY'VE BEEN SEEN IN THIS AREA.
HO, HO, HO! WE'RE LOOKING FOR THEM TOO. THEY'RE GOTHS FROM THE WEST WHO ARE IN THE EAST!
?!
A VISIGOTH HELMET! YOU'RE A HORDE OF GOTHS!!!
WHO, US?
CALL THAT A HORDE, DECURION? THERE'S ONLY TWO OF THEM!
SHALL WE GET THEM, ASTERIX!
LET'S GET THEM, OBELIX!
PAF!
IT WAS A GOOD IDEA TO DRINK SOME OF THAT POTION!
COME ON, YOU ROMANS! DO SOMETHING! PUT UP A FIGHT!
SOON AFTERWARDS...
YOU WERE RIGHT, DECURION, THAT WAS A HORDE!
11

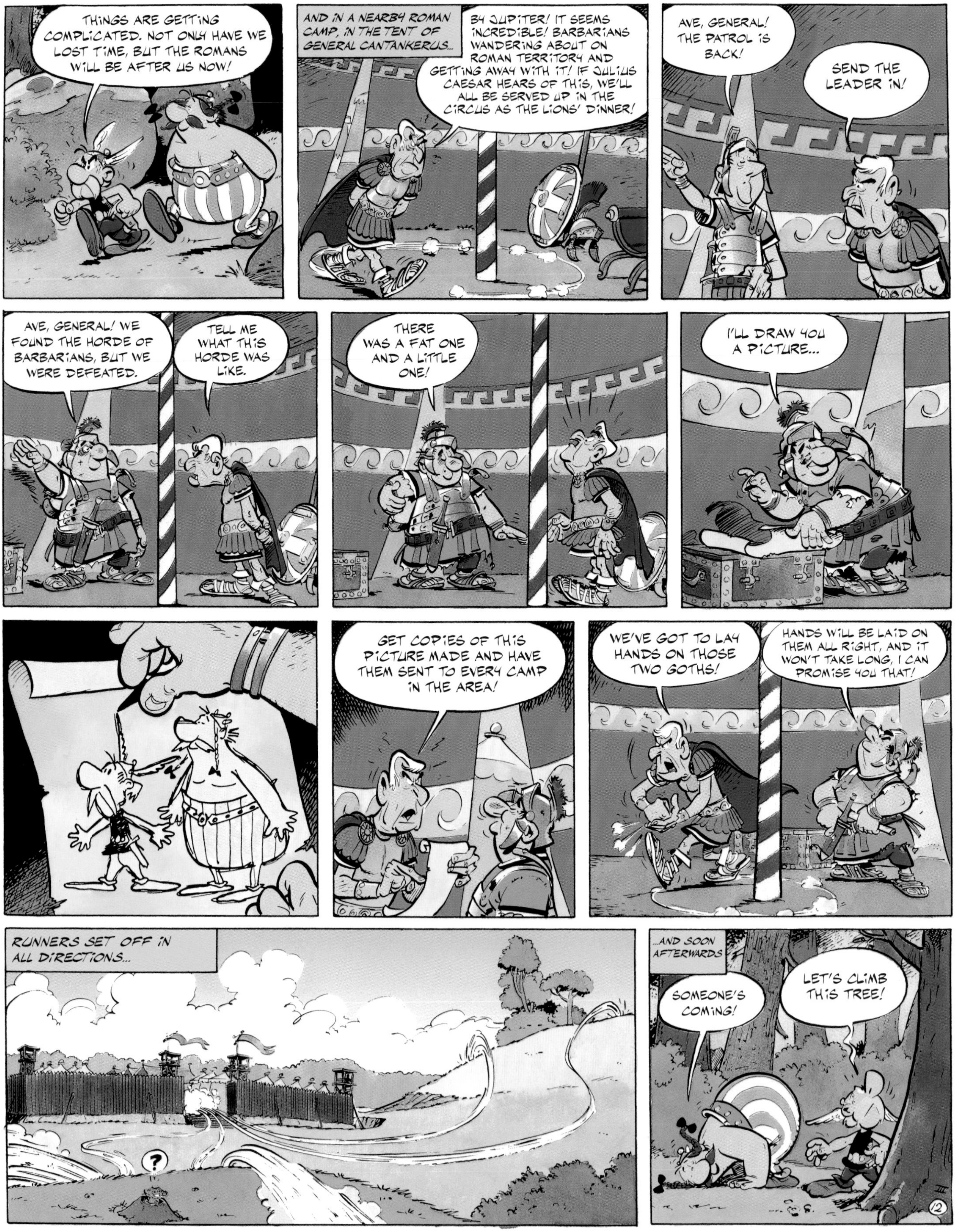
THINGS ARE GETTING COMPLICATED. NOT ONLY HAVE WE LOST TIME, BUT THE ROMANS WILL BE AFTER US NOW!
AND IN A NEARBY ROMAN CAMP, IN THE TENT OF GENERAL CANTANKERUS...
BY JUPITER! IT SEEMS INCREDIBLE! BARBARIANS WANDERING ABOUT ON ROMAN TERRITORY AND GETTING AWAY WITH IT! IF JULIUS CAESAR HEARS OF THIS, WE'LL ALL BE SERVED UP IN THE CIRCUS AS THE LIONS' DINNER!
AVE, GENERAL! THE PATROL IS BACK!
SEND THE LEADER IN!
AVE, GENERAL! WE FOUND THE HORDE OF BARBARIANS, BUT WE WERE DEFEATED.
TELL ME WHAT THIS HORDE WAS LIKE.
THERE WAS A FAT ONE AND A LITTLE ONE!
I'LL DRAW YOU A PICTURE...
GET COPIES OF THIS PICTURE MADE AND HAVE THEM SENT TO EVERY CAMP IN THE AREA!
WE'VE GOT TO LAY HANDS ON THOSE TWO GOTHS!
HANDS WILL BE LAID ON THEM ALL RIGHT, AND IT WON'T TAKE LONG, I CAN PROMISE YOU THAT!
RUNNERS SET OFF IN ALL DIRECTIONS...
?
...AND SOON AFTERWARDS
SOMEONE'S COMING!
LET'S CLIMB THIS TREE!
12

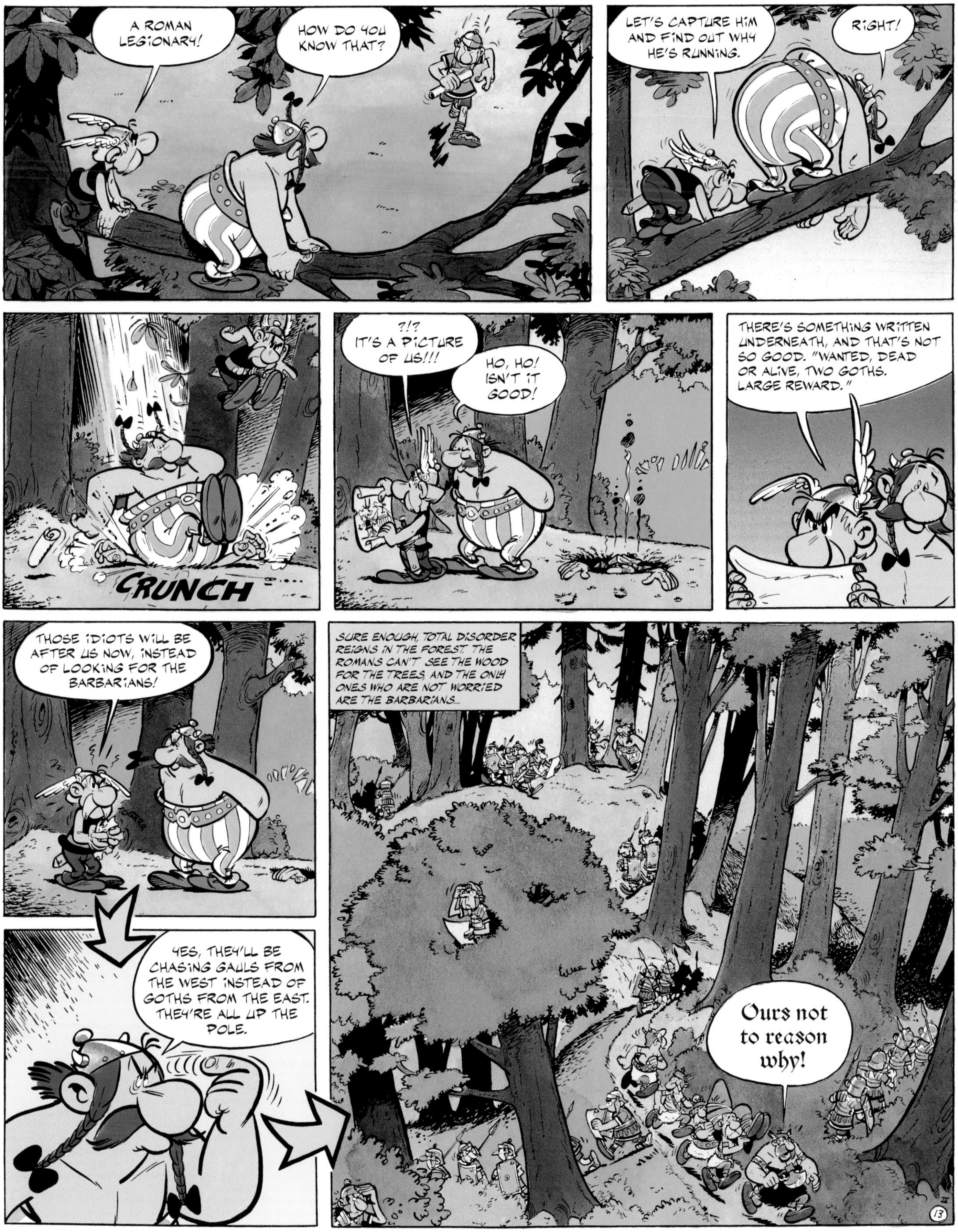

A ROMAN LEGIONARY!
HOW DO YOU KNOW THAT?
LET'S CAPTURE HIM AND FIND OUT WHY HE'S RUNNING.
RIGHT!
CRUNCH
?!? IT'S A PICTURE OF US!!!
HO, HO! ISN'T IT GOOD!
THERE'S SOMETHING WRITTEN UNDERNEATH, AND THAT'S NOT SO GOOD. "WANTED, DEAD OR ALIVE, TWO GOTHS. LARGE REWARD."
THOSE IDIOTS WILL BE AFTER US NOW, INSTEAD OF LOOKING FOR THE BARBARIANS!
YES, THEY'LL BE CHASING GAULS FROM THE WEST INSTEAD OF GOTHS FROM THE EAST. THEY'RE ALL UP THE POLE.
SURE ENOUGH, TOTAL DISORDER REIGNS IN THE FOREST. THE ROMANS CAN'T SEE THE WOOD FOR THE TREES AND THE ONLY ONES WHO ARE NOT WORRIED ARE THE BARBARIANS...
Ours not to reason why!
13

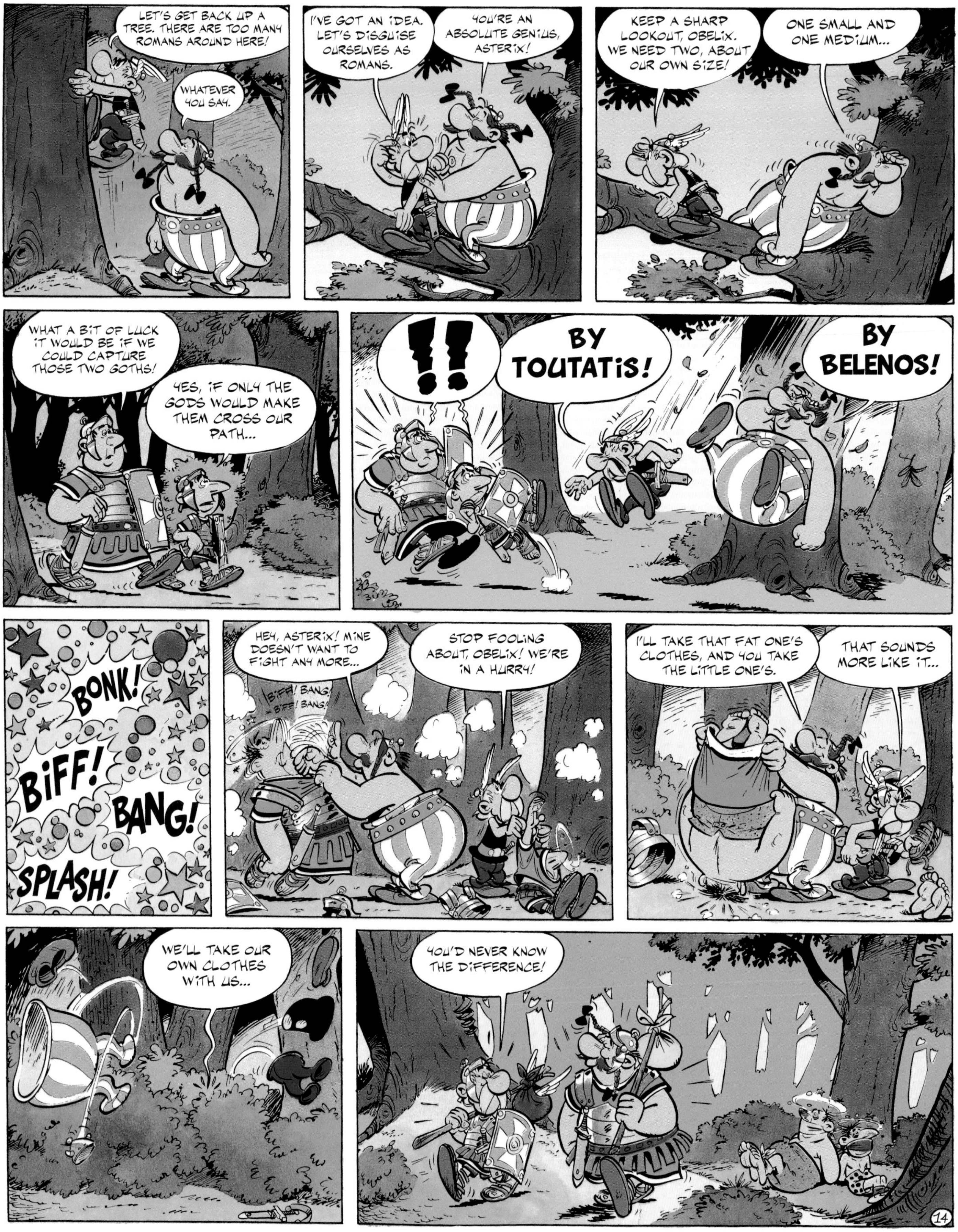
LET'S GET BACK UP A TREE. THERE ARE TOO MANY ROMANS AROUND HERE!
WHATEVER YOU SAY.
I'VE GOT AN IDEA. LET'S DISGUISE OURSELVES AS ROMANS.
YOU'RE AN ABSOLUTE GENIUS, ASTERIX!
KEEP A SHARP LOOKOUT, OBELIX. WE NEED TWO, ABOUT OUR OWN SIZE!
ONE SMALL AND ONE MEDIUM...
WHAT A BIT OF LUCK IT WOULD BE IF WE COULD CAPTURE THOSE TWO GOTHS!
YES, IF ONLY THE GODS WOULD MAKE THEM CROSS OUR PATH...
!!
BY TOUTATIS!
BY BELENOS!
BONK!
BIFF!
BANG!
SPLASH!
HEY, ASTERIX! MINE DOESN'T WANT TO FIGHT ANY MORE...
BIFF! BANG!
BIFF! BANG!
STOP FOOLING ABOUT, OBELIX! WE'RE IN A HURRY!
I'LL TAKE THAT FAT ONE'S CLOTHES, AND YOU TAKE THE LITTLE ONE'S.
THAT SOUNDS MORE LIKE IT...
WE'LL TAKE OUR OWN CLOTHES WITH US...
YOU'D NEVER KNOW THE DIFFERENCE!
14

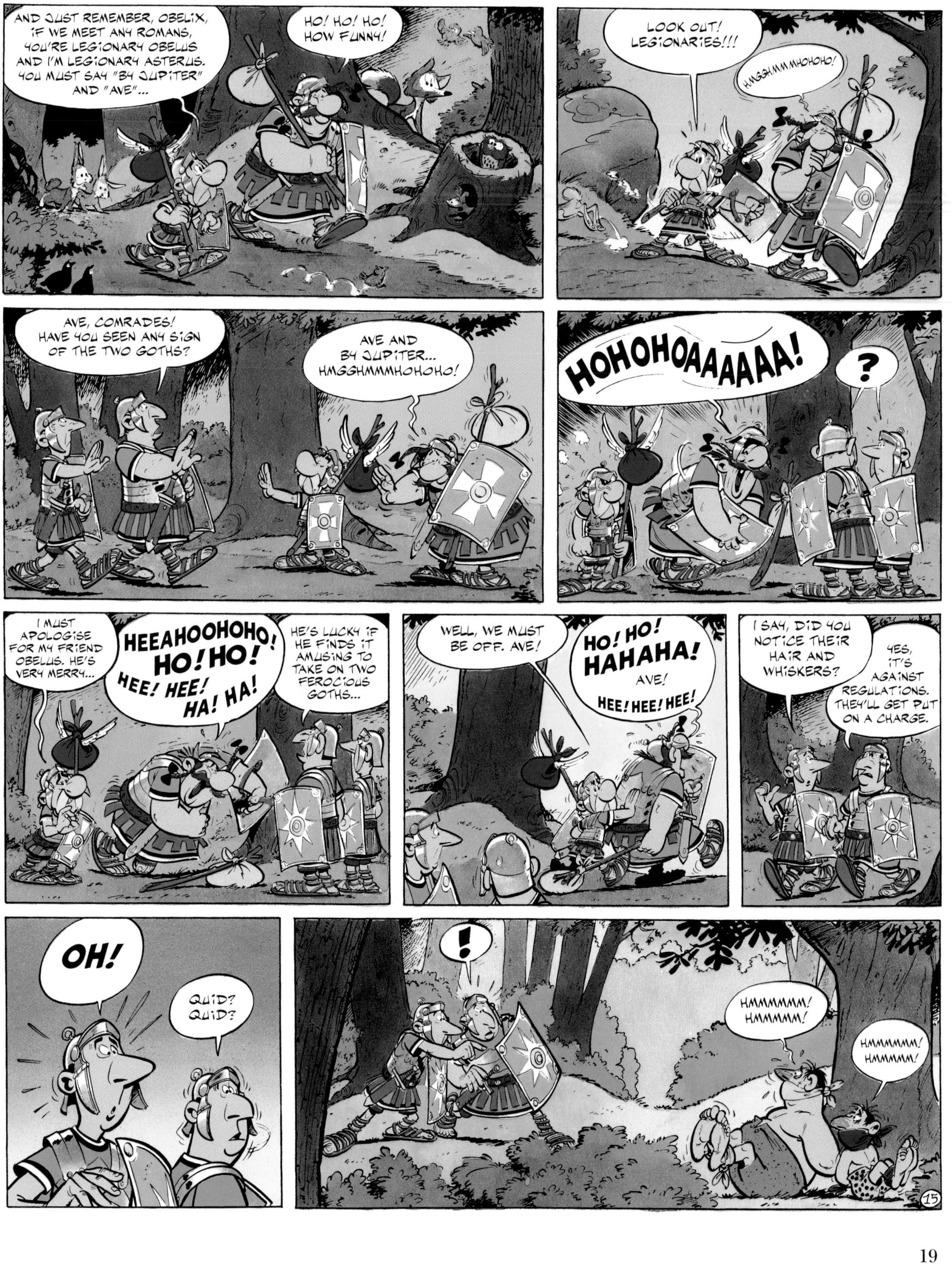
AND JUST REMEMBER, OBELIX, IF WE MEET ANY ROMANS, YOU'RE LEGIONARY OBELUS AND I'M LEGIONARY ASTERUS. YOU MUST SAY "BY JUPITER" AND "AVE"...
HO! HO! HO! HOW FUNNY!
LOOK OUT! LEGIONARIES!!!
HMGGHMMMHOHOHO!
AVE, COMRADES! HAVE YOU SEEN ANY SIGN OF THE TWO GOTHS?
AVE AND BY JUPITER... HMGGHMMMHOHOHO!
HOHOHOAAAAAA!
?
I MUST APOLOGISE FOR MY FRIEND OBELUS. HE'S VERY MERRY...
HEEAHOOHOHO! HO! HO! HEE! HEE! HA! HA!
HE'S LUCKY IF HE FINDS IT AMUSING TO TAKE ON TWO FEROCIOUS GOTHS...
WELL, WE MUST BE OFF. AVE!
HO! HO! HAHAHA! AVE! HEE! HEE! HEE!
I SAY, DID YOU NOTICE THEIR HAIR AND WHISKERS?
YES, IT'S AGAINST REGULATIONS. THEY'LL GET PUT ON A CHARGE.
OH!
QUID? QUID?
!
HMMMMMM! HMMMMM!
HMMMMMM! HMMMMM!
15

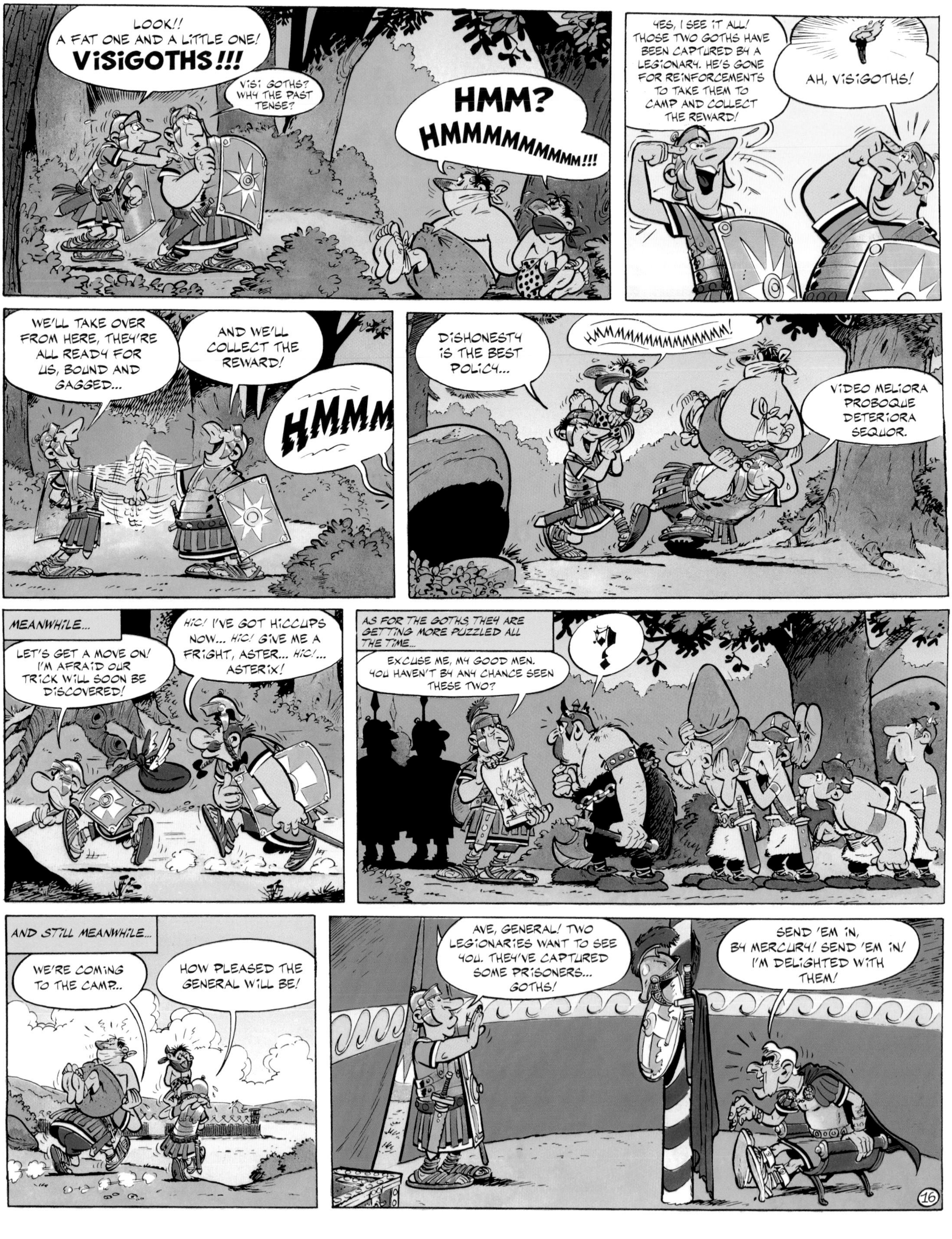
LOOK!! A FAT ONE AND A LITTLE ONE! VISIGOTHS!!!
VISI GOTHS? WHY THE PAST TENSE?
HMM? HMMMMMMMMM!!!
YES, I SEE IT ALL! THOSE TWO GOTHS HAVE BEEN CAPTURED BY A LEGIONARY. HE'S GONE FOR REINFORCEMENTS TO TAKE THEM TO CAMP AND COLLECT THE REWARD!
AH, VISIGOTHS!
WE'LL TAKE OVER FROM HERE, THEY'RE ALL READY FOR US, BOUND AND GAGGED...
AND WE'LL COLLECT THE REWARD!
HMMM
DISHONESTY IS THE BEST POLICY...
HMMMMMMMMMMMMMM!
VIDEO MELIORA PROBOQUE DETERIORA SEQUOR.
MEANWHILE...
LET'S GET A MOVE ON! I'M AFRAID OUR TRICK WILL SOON BE DISCOVERED!
HIC! I'VE GOT HICCUPS NOW... HIC! GIVE ME A FRIGHT, ASTER... HIC!... ASTERIX!
AS FOR THE GOTHS THEY ARE GETTING MORE PUZZLED ALL THE TIME...
EXCUSE ME, MY GOOD MEN. YOU HAVEN'T BY ANY CHANCE SEEN THESE TWO?
AND STILL MEANWHILE...
WE'RE COMING TO THE CAMP...
HOW PLEASED THE GENERAL WILL BE!
AVE, GENERAL! TWO LEGIONARIES WANT TO SEE YOU. THEY'VE CAPTURED SOME PRISONERS... GOTHS!
SEND 'EM IN, BY MERCURY! SEND 'EM IN! I'M DELIGHTED WITH THEM!
16

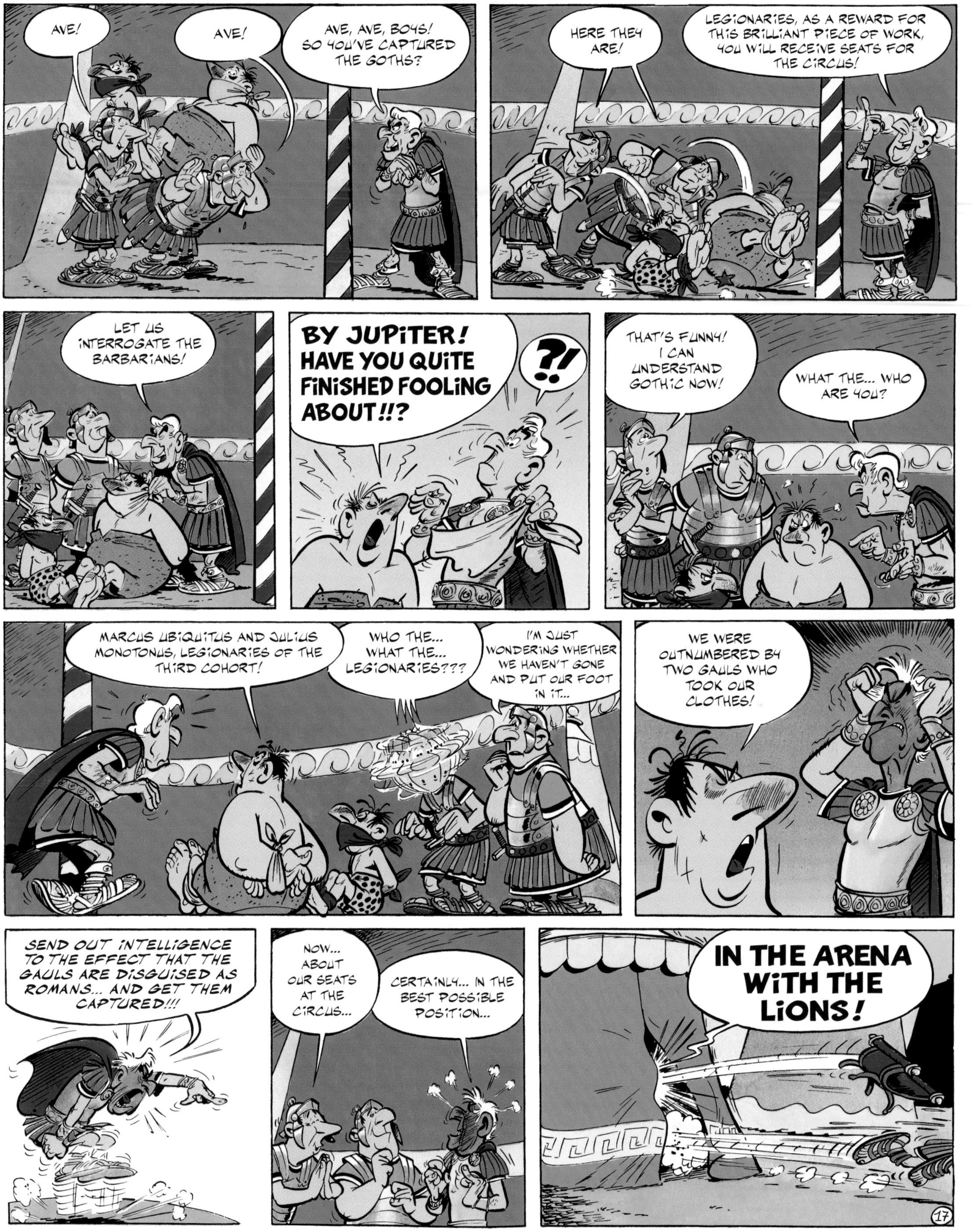
AVE!
AVE!
AVE, AVE, BOYS! SO YOU'VE CAPTURED THE GOTHS?
HERE THEY ARE!
LEGIONARIES, AS A REWARD FOR THIS BRILLIANT PIECE OF WORK, YOU WILL RECEIVE SEATS FOR THE CIRCUS!
LET US INTERROGATE THE BARBARIANS!
BY JUPITER! HAVE YOU QUITE FINISHED FOOLING ABOUT!!?
?!
THAT'S FUNNY! I CAN UNDERSTAND GOTHIC NOW!
WHAT THE... WHO ARE YOU?
MARCUS UBIQUITUS AND JULIUS MONOTONUS, LEGIONARIES OF THE THIRD COHORT!
WHO THE... WHAT THE... LEGIONARIES???
I'M JUST WONDERING WHETHER WE HAVEN'T GONE AND PUT OUR FOOT IN IT...
WE WERE OUTNUMBERED BY TWO GAULS WHO TOOK OUR CLOTHES!
SEND OUT INTELLIGENCE TO THE EFFECT THAT THE GAULS ARE DISGUISED AS ROMANS... AND GET THEM CAPTURED!!!
NOW... ABOUT OUR SEATS AT THE CIRCUS...
CERTAINLY... IN THE BEST POSSIBLE POSITION...
IN THE ARENA WITH THE LIONS!
17

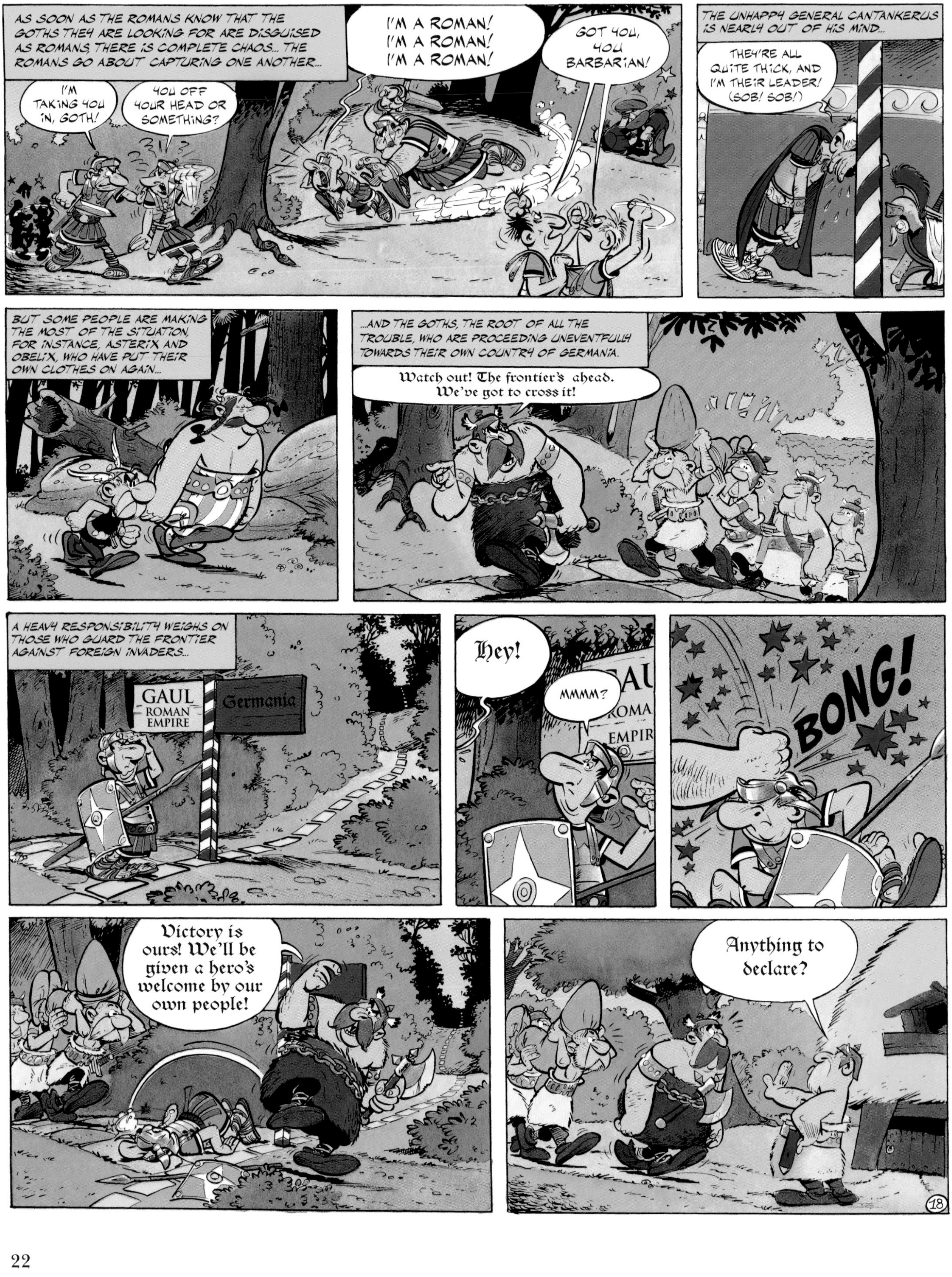
AS SOON AS THE ROMANS KNOW THAT THE GOTHS THEY ARE LOOKING FOR ARE DISGUISED AS ROMANS, THERE IS COMPLETE CHAOS... THE ROMANS GO ABOUT CAPTURING ONE ANOTHER...
I'M TAKING YOU IN, GOTH!
YOU OFF YOUR HEAD OR SOMETHING?
I'M A ROMAN! I'M A ROMAN! I'M A ROMAN!
GOT YOU, YOU BARBARIAN!
THE UNHAPPY GENERAL CANTANKERUS IS NEARLY OUT OF HIS MIND...
THEY'RE ALL QUITE THICK, AND I'M THEIR LEADER! (SOB! SOB!)
BUT SOME PEOPLE ARE MAKING THE MOST OF THE SITUATION, FOR INSTANCE, ASTERIX AND OBELIX, WHO HAVE PUT THEIR OWN CLOTHES ON AGAIN...
...AND THE GOTHS, THE ROOT OF ALL THE TROUBLE, WHO ARE PROCEEDING UNEVENTFULLY TOWARDS THEIR OWN COUNTRY OF GERMANIA.
Watch out! The frontier's ahead. We've got to cross it!
A HEAVY RESPONSIBILITY WEIGHS ON THOSE WHO GUARD THE FRONTIER AGAINST FOREIGN INVADERS...
GAUL ROMAN EMPIRE
Germania
Hey!
MMMM?
BONG!
Victory is ours! We'll be given a hero's welcome by our own people!
Anything to declare?
18

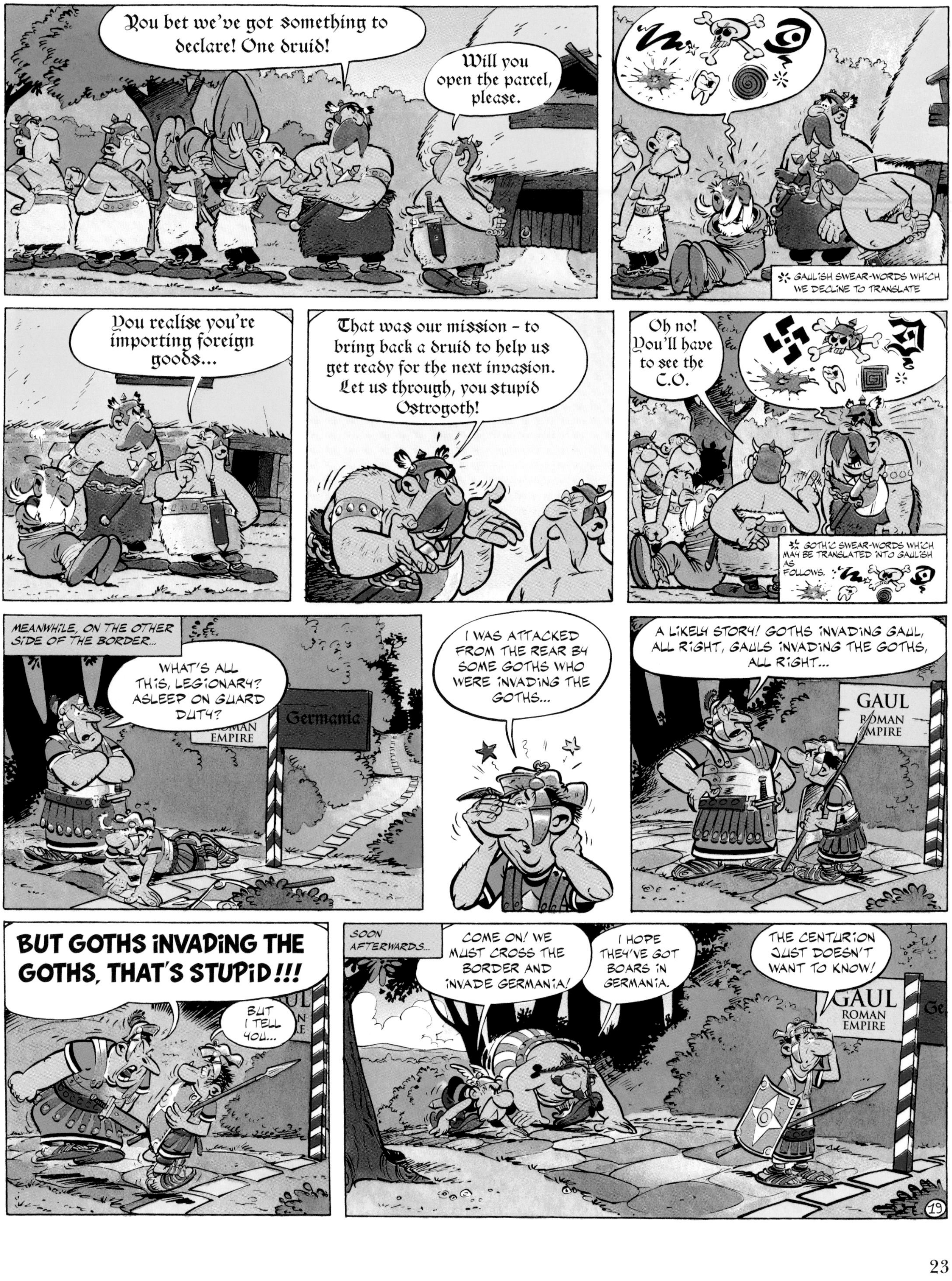
You bet we've got something to declare! One druid!
Will you open the parcel, please.
* GAULISH SWEAR-WORDS WHICH WE DECLINE TO TRANSLATE
You realise you're importing foreign goods...
That was our mission – to bring back a druid to help us get ready for the next invasion. Let us through, you stupid Ostrogoth!
Oh no! You'll have to see the C.O.
* GOTHIC SWEAR-WORDS WHICH MAY BE TRANSLATED INTO GAULISH AS FOLLOWS.
MEANWHILE, ON THE OTHER SIDE OF THE BORDER...
WHAT'S ALL THIS, LEGIONARY? ASLEEP ON GUARD DUTY?
ROMAN EMPIRE
Germania
I WAS ATTACKED FROM THE REAR BY SOME GOTHS WHO WERE INVADING THE GOTHS...
A LIKELY STORY! GOTHS INVADING GAUL, ALL RIGHT, GAULS INVADING THE GOTHS, ALL RIGHT...
GAUL
ROMAN EMPIRE
BUT GOTHS INVADING THE GOTHS, THAT'S STUPID!!!
BUT I TELL YOU...
SOON AFTERWARDS...
COME ON! WE MUST CROSS THE BORDER AND INVADE GERMANIA!
I HOPE THEY'VE GOT BOARS IN GERMANIA.
THE CENTURION JUST DOESN'T WANT TO KNOW!
GAUL
ROMAN EMPIRE
19

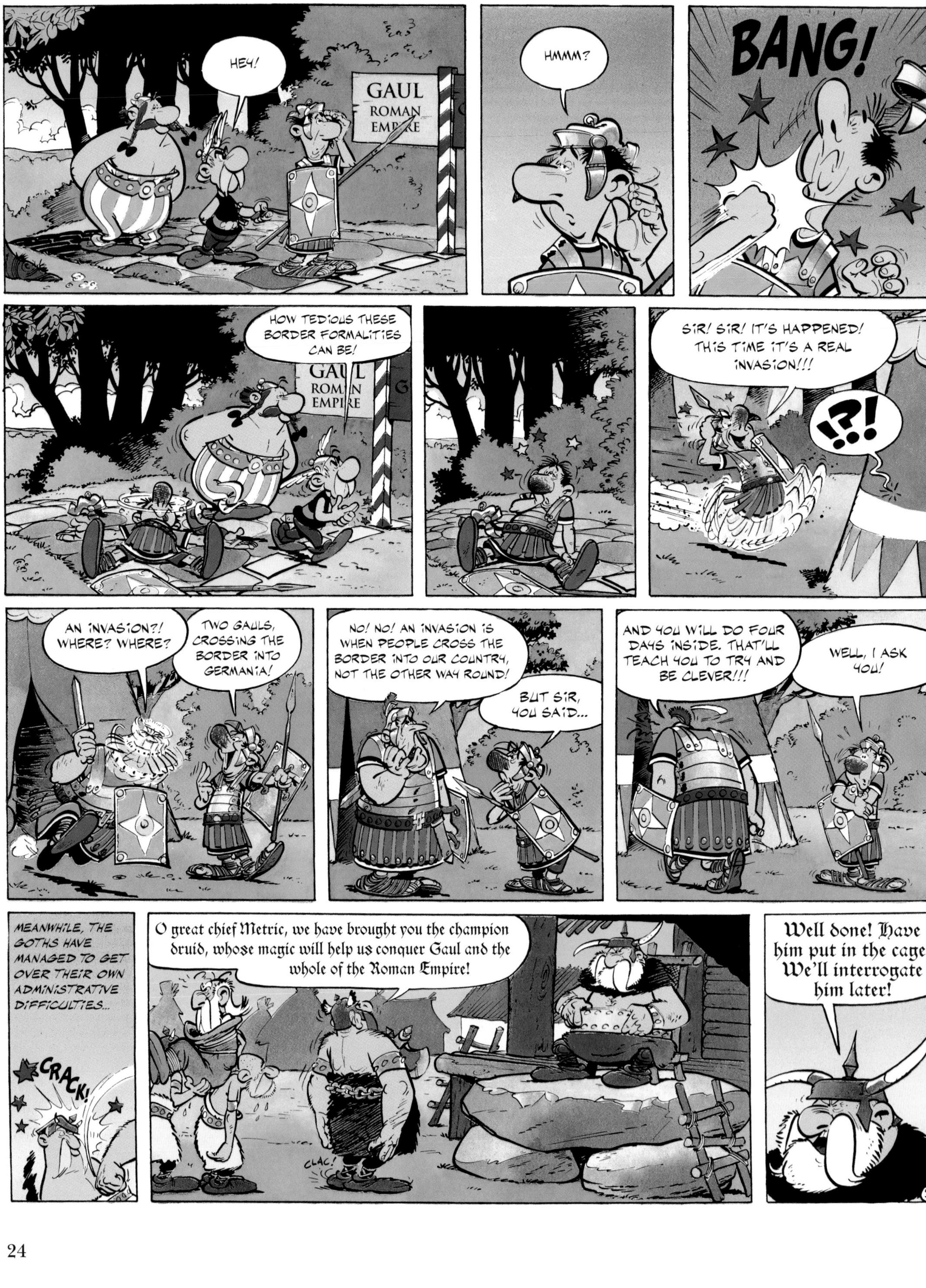
HEY!
GAUL
ROMAN EMPIRE
HMMM?
BANG!
HOW TEDIOUS THESE BORDER FORMALITIES CAN BE!
GAUL
ROMAN EMPIRE
SIR! SIR! IT'S HAPPENED! THIS TIME IT'S A REAL INVASION!!!
!?!
AN INVASION?! WHERE? WHERE?
TWO GAULS, CROSSING THE BORDER INTO GERMANIA!
NO! NO! AN INVASION IS WHEN PEOPLE CROSS THE BORDER INTO OUR COUNTRY, NOT THE OTHER WAY ROUND!
BUT SIR, YOU SAID...
AND YOU WILL DO FOUR DAYS INSIDE. THAT'LL TEACH YOU TO TRY AND BE CLEVER!!!
WELL, I ASK YOU!
MEANWHILE, THE GOTHS HAVE MANAGED TO GET OVER THEIR OWN ADMINISTRATIVE DIFFICULTIES...
CRACK!
O great chief Metric, we have brought you the champion druid, whose magic will help us conquer Gaul and the whole of the Roman Empire!
CLAC!
Well done! Have him put in the cage. We'll interrogate him later!
20

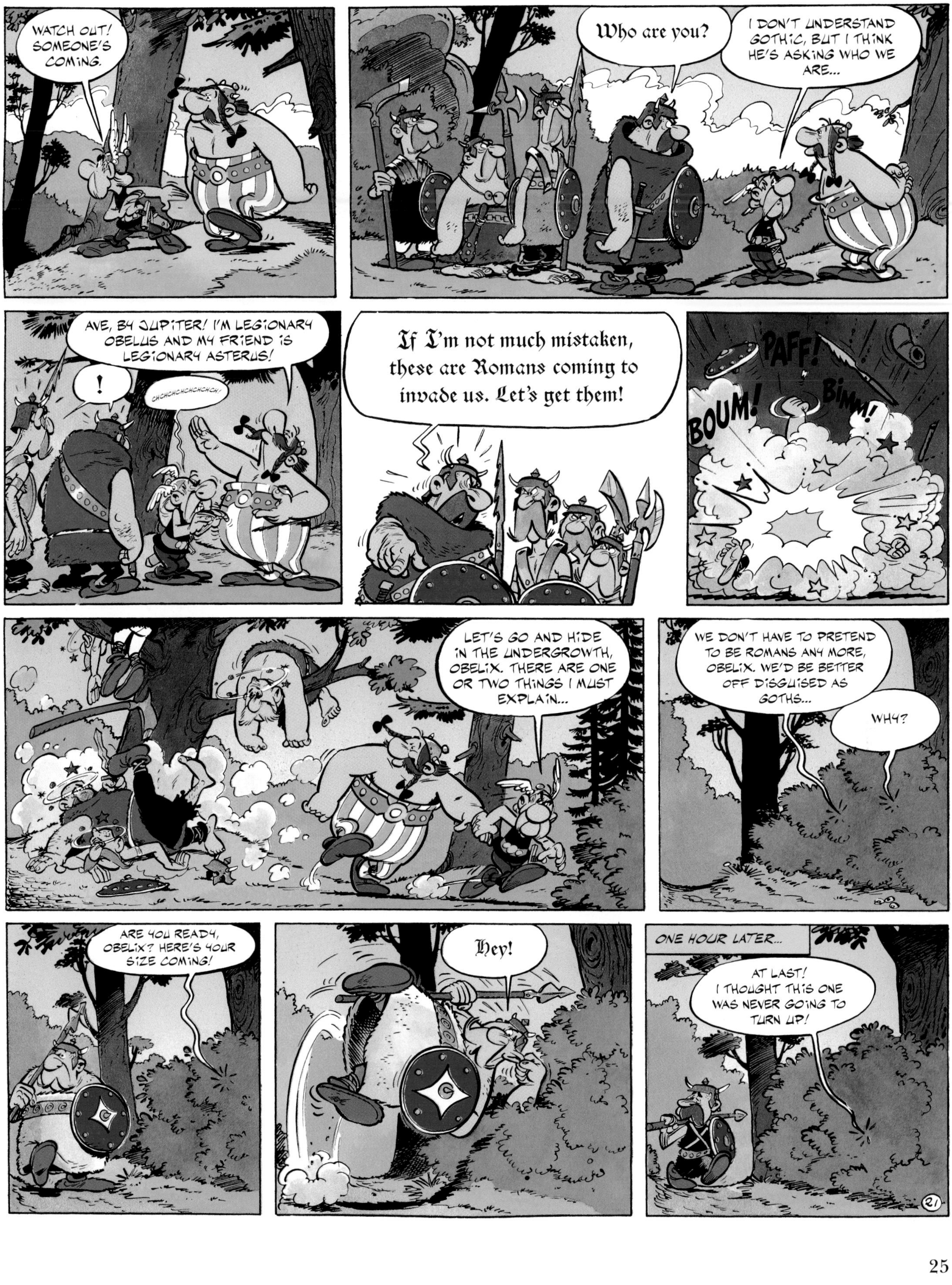
WATCH OUT! SOMEONE'S COMING.
Who are you?
I DON'T UNDERSTAND GOTHIC, BUT I THINK HE'S ASKING WHO WE ARE...
AVE, BY JUPITER! I'M LEGIONARY OBELUS AND MY FRIEND IS LEGIONARY ASTERUS!
!
If I'm not much mistaken, these are Romans coming to invade us. Let's get them!
PAFF!
BIMM!
BOUM!
LET'S GO AND HIDE IN THE UNDERGROWTH, OBELIX. THERE ARE ONE OR TWO THINGS I MUST EXPLAIN...
WE DON'T HAVE TO PRETEND TO BE ROMANS ANY MORE, OBELIX. WE'D BE BETTER OFF DISGUISED AS GOTHS...
WHY?
ARE YOU READY, OBELIX? HERE'S YOUR SIZE COMING!
Hey!
ONE HOUR LATER...
AT LAST! I THOUGHT THIS ONE WAS NEVER GOING TO TURN UP!
21

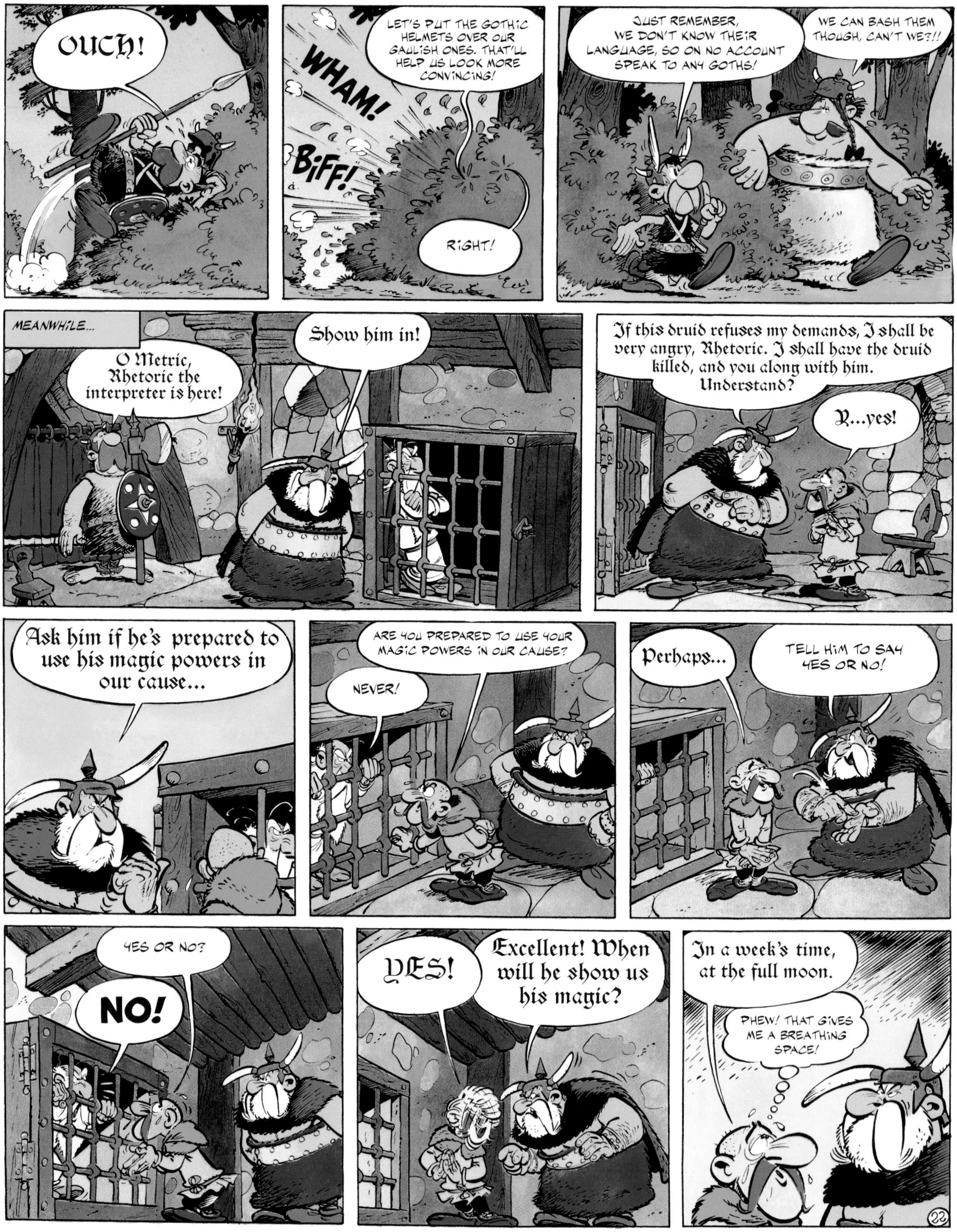

OUCH!
LET'S PUT THE GOTHIC HELMETS OVER OUR GAULISH ONES. THAT'LL HELP US LOOK MORE CONVINCING!
WHAM!
BIFF!
RIGHT!
JUST REMEMBER, WE DON'T KNOW THEIR LANGUAGE, SO ON NO ACCOUNT SPEAK TO ANY GOTHS!
WE CAN BASH THEM THOUGH, CAN'T WE?!!
MEANWHILE...
O Metric, Rhetoric the interpreter is here!
Show him in!
If this druid refuses my demands, I shall be very angry, Rhetoric. I shall have the druid killed, and you along with him. Understand?
Y...yes!
Ask him if he's prepared to use his magic powers in our cause...
ARE YOU PREPARED TO USE YOUR MAGIC POWERS IN OUR CAUSE?
NEVER!
Perhaps...
TELL HIM TO SAY YES OR NO!
YES OR NO?
NO!
YES!
Excellent! When will he show us his magic?
In a week's time, at the full moon.
PHEW! THAT GIVES ME A BREATHING SPACE!
22

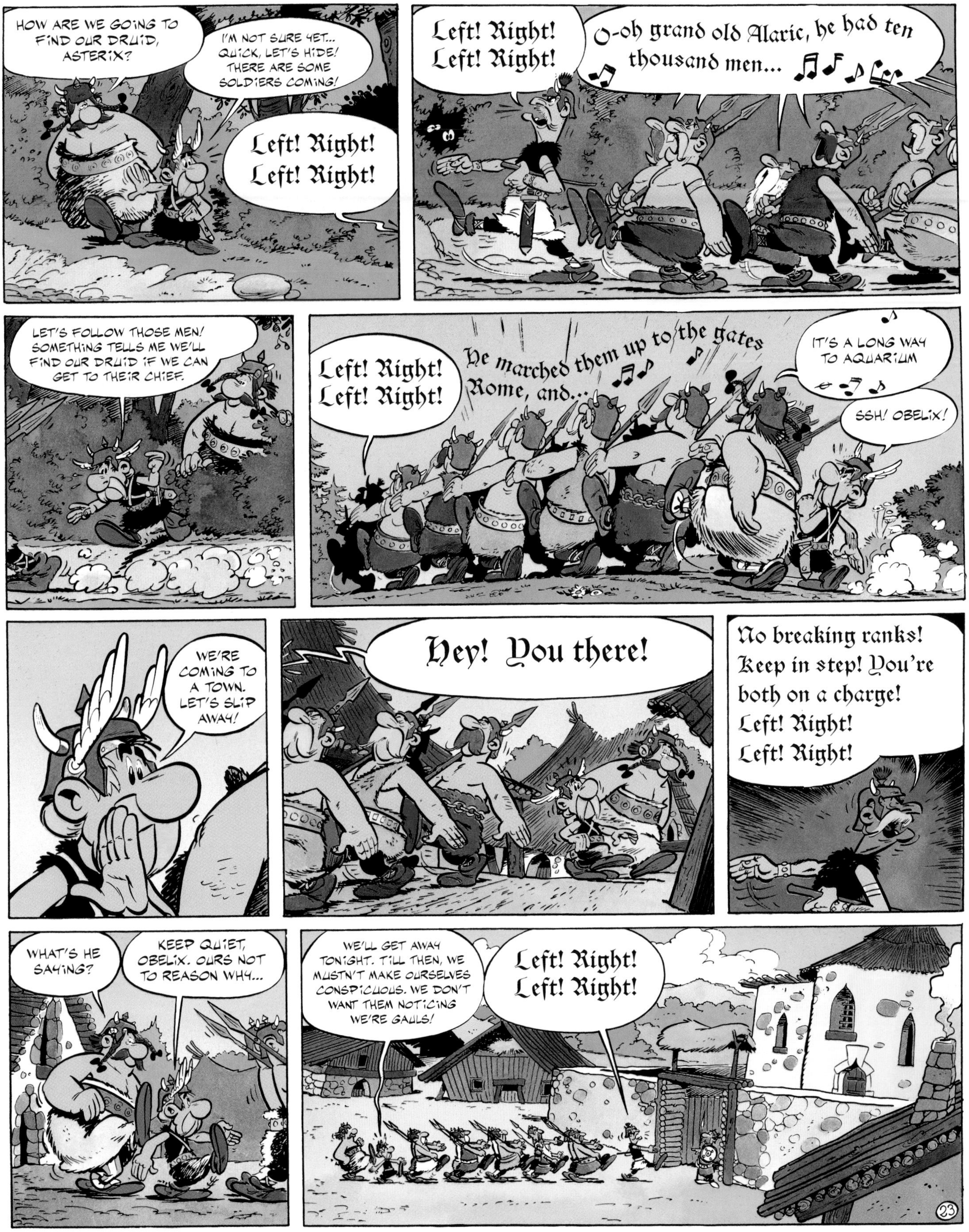
HOW ARE WE GOING TO FIND OUR DRUID, ASTERIX?
I'M NOT SURE YET... QUICK, LET'S HIDE! THERE ARE SOME SOLDIERS COMING!
Left! Right! Left! Right!
Left! Right! Left! Right!
O-oh grand old Alaric, he had ten thousand men...
LET'S FOLLOW THOSE MEN! SOMETHING TELLS ME WE'LL FIND OUR DRUID IF WE CAN GET TO THEIR CHIEF.
Left! Right! Left! Right!
He marched them up to the gates of Rome, and...
IT'S A LONG WAY TO AQUARIUM
SSH! OBELIX!
WE'RE COMING TO A TOWN. LET'S SLIP AWAY!
Hey! You there!
No breaking ranks! Keep in step! You're both on a charge! Left! Right! Left! Right!
WHAT'S HE SAYING?
KEEP QUIET, OBELIX. OURS NOT TO REASON WHY...
WE'LL GET AWAY TONIGHT. TILL THEN, WE MUSTN'T MAKE OURSELVES CONSPICUOUS. WE DON'T WANT THEM NOTICING WE'RE GAULS!
Left! Right! Left! Right!
23

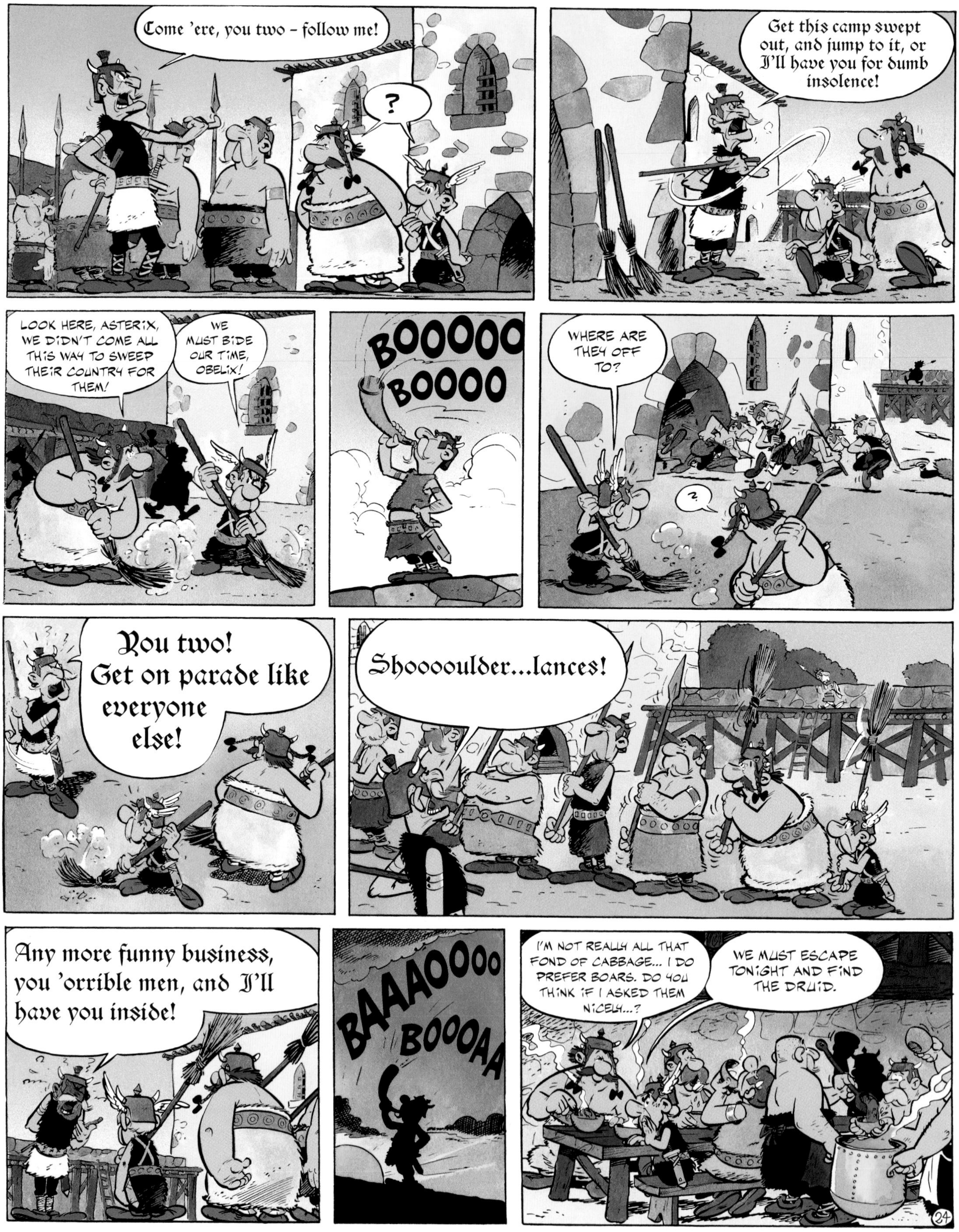
Come 'ere, you two – follow me!
?
Get this camp swept out, and jump to it, or I'll have you for dumb insolence!
LOOK HERE, ASTERIX, WE DIDN'T COME ALL THIS WAY TO SWEEP THEIR COUNTRY FOR THEM!
WE MUST BIDE OUR TIME, OBELIX!
BOOOOO BOOOO
WHERE ARE THEY OFF TO?
?
You two! Get on parade like everyone else!
Shooooulder...lances!
Any more funny business, you 'orrible men, and I'll have you inside!
BAAAOOOO BOOOAA
I'M NOT REALLY ALL THAT FOND OF CABBAGE... I DO PREFER BOARS. DO YOU THINK IF I ASKED THEM NICELY...?
WE MUST ESCAPE TONIGHT AND FIND THE DRUID.
24

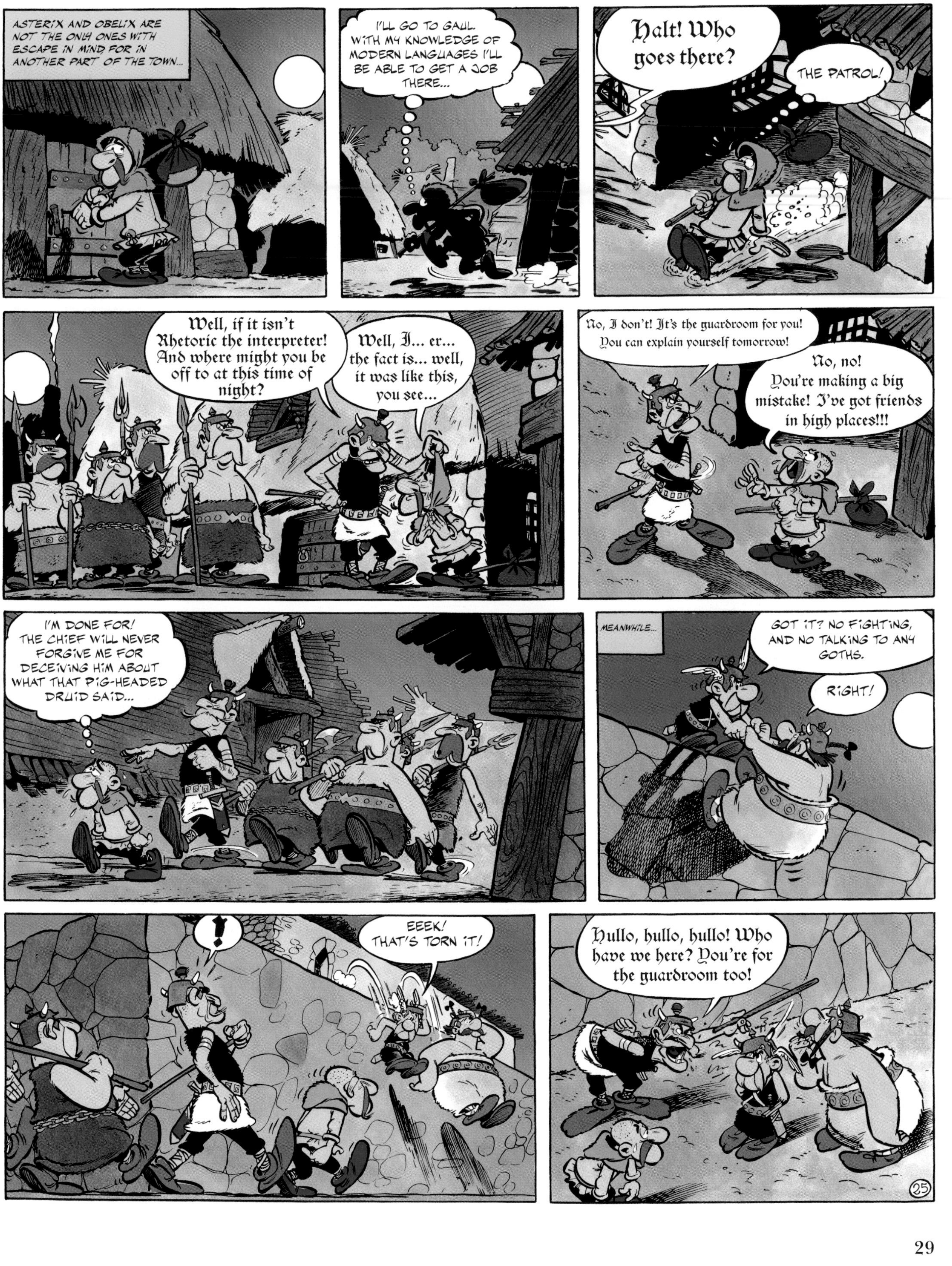
ASTERIX AND OBELIX ARE NOT THE ONLY ONES WITH ESCAPE IN MIND FOR IN ANOTHER PART OF THE TOWN...
I'LL GO TO GAUL. WITH MY KNOWLEDGE OF MODERN LANGUAGES I'LL BE ABLE TO GET A JOB THERE...
Halt! Who goes there?
THE PATROL!
Well, if it isn't Rhetoric the interpreter! And where might you be off to at this time of night?
Well, I... er... the fact is... well, it was like this, you see...
No, I don't! It's the guardroom for you! You can explain yourself tomorrow!
No, no! You're making a big mistake! I've got friends in high places!!!
I'M DONE FOR! THE CHIEF WILL NEVER FORGIVE ME FOR DECEIVING HIM ABOUT WHAT THAT PIG-HEADED DRUID SAID...
MEANWHILE...
GOT IT? NO FIGHTING, AND NO TALKING TO ANY GOTHS.
RIGHT!
!
EEEK! THAT'S TORN IT!
Hullo, hullo, hullo! Who have we here? You're for the guardroom too!
25

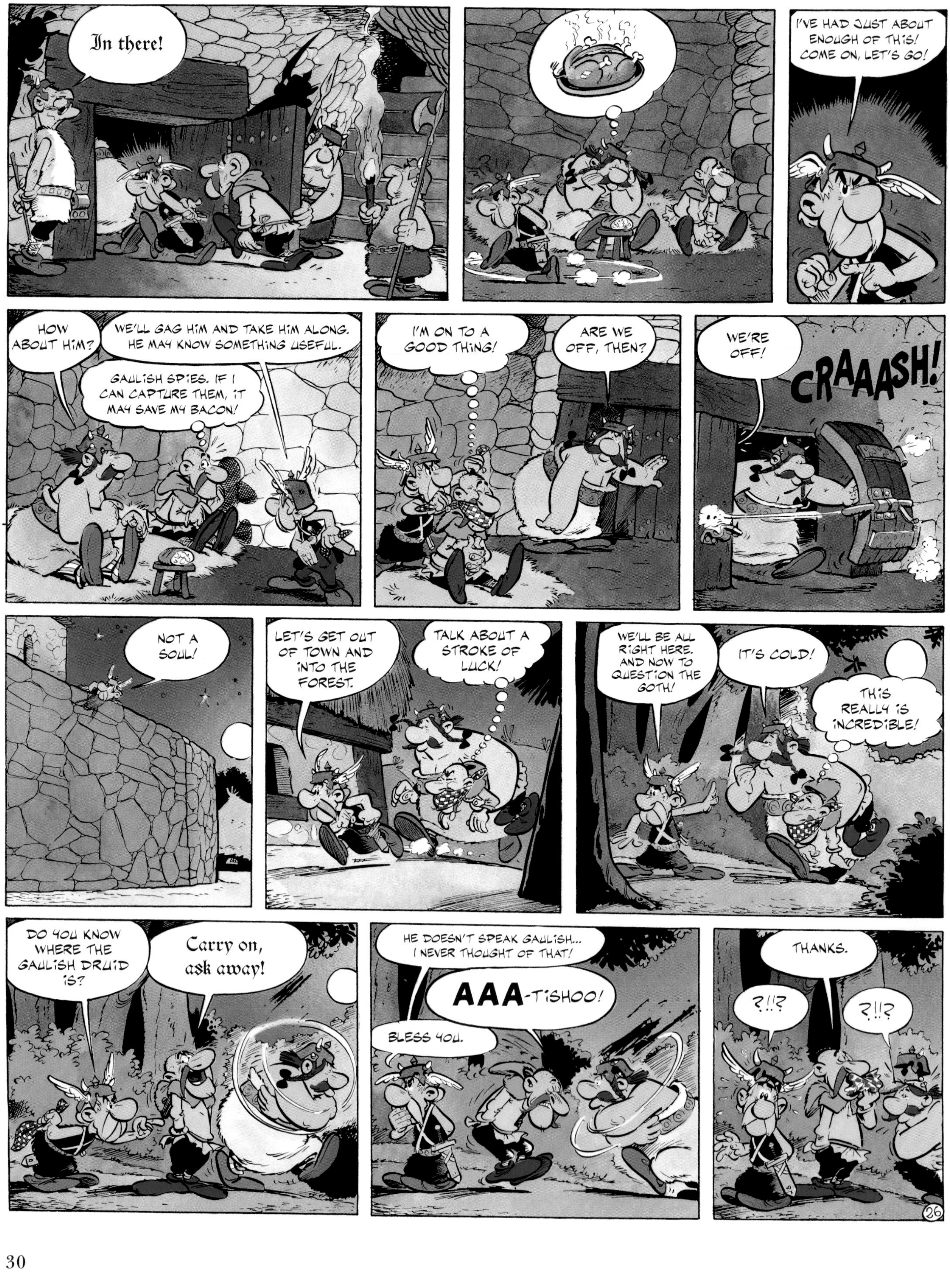
In there!
I'VE HAD JUST ABOUT ENOUGH OF THIS! COME ON, LET'S GO!
HOW ABOUT HIM?
WE'LL GAG HIM AND TAKE HIM ALONG. HE MAY KNOW SOMETHING USEFUL.
GAULISH SPIES. IF I CAN CAPTURE THEM, IT MAY SAVE MY BACON!
I'M ON TO A GOOD THING!
ARE WE OFF, THEN?
WE'RE OFF!
CRAAASH!
NOT A SOUL!
LET'S GET OUT OF TOWN AND INTO THE FOREST.
TALK ABOUT A STROKE OF LUCK!
WE'LL BE ALL RIGHT HERE. AND NOW TO QUESTION THE GOTH!
IT'S COLD!
THIS REALLY IS INCREDIBLE!
DO YOU KNOW WHERE THE GAULISH DRUID IS?
Carry on, ask away!
HE DOESN'T SPEAK GAULISH... I NEVER THOUGHT OF THAT!
AAA-TISHOO!
BLESS YOU.
THANKS.
?!!?
?!!?
26

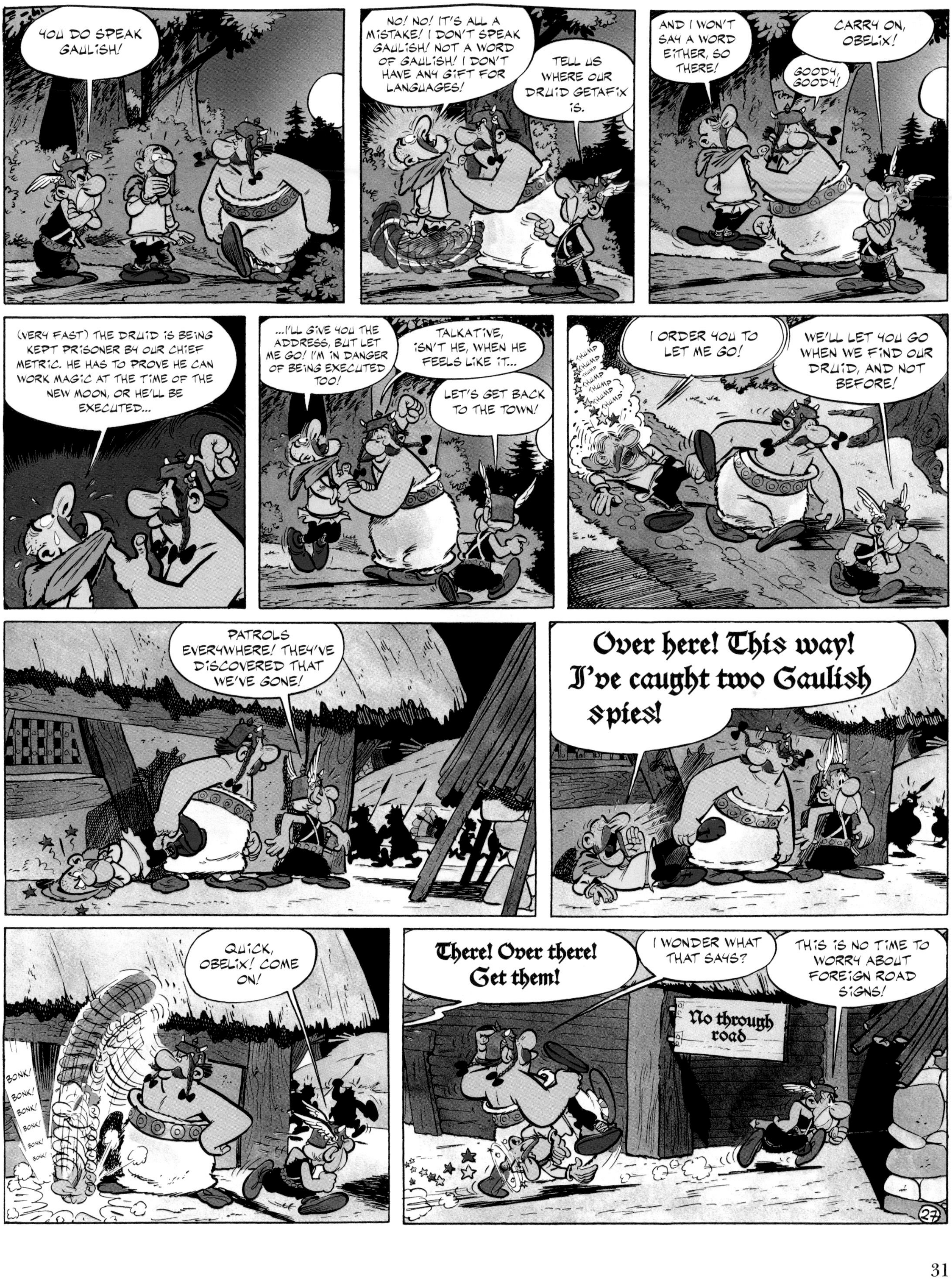
YOU DO SPEAK GAULISH!
NO! NO! IT'S ALL A MISTAKE! I DON'T SPEAK GAULISH! NOT A WORD OF GAULISH! I DON'T HAVE ANY GIFT FOR LANGUAGES!
TELL US WHERE OUR DRUID GETAFIX IS.
AND I WON'T SAY A WORD EITHER, SO THERE!
CARRY ON, OBELIX!
GOODY, GOODY!
(VERY FAST) THE DRUID IS BEING KEPT PRISONER BY OUR CHIEF METRIC. HE HAS TO PROVE HE CAN WORK MAGIC AT THE TIME OF THE NEW MOON, OR HE'LL BE EXECUTED...
...I'LL GIVE YOU THE ADDRESS, BUT LET ME GO! I'M IN DANGER OF BEING EXECUTED TOO!
TALKATIVE, ISN'T HE, WHEN HE FEELS LIKE IT...
LET'S GET BACK TO THE TOWN!
I ORDER YOU TO LET ME GO!
WE'LL LET YOU GO WHEN WE FIND OUR DRUID, AND NOT BEFORE!
PATROLS EVERYWHERE! THEY'VE DISCOVERED THAT WE'VE GONE!
Over here! This way! I've caught two Gaulish spies!
QUICK, OBELIX! COME ON!
BONK! BONK! BONK! BONK! BONK! BONK!
There! Over there! Get them!
I WONDER WHAT THAT SAYS?
THIS IS NO TIME TO WORRY ABOUT FOREIGN ROAD SIGNS!
No through road
27

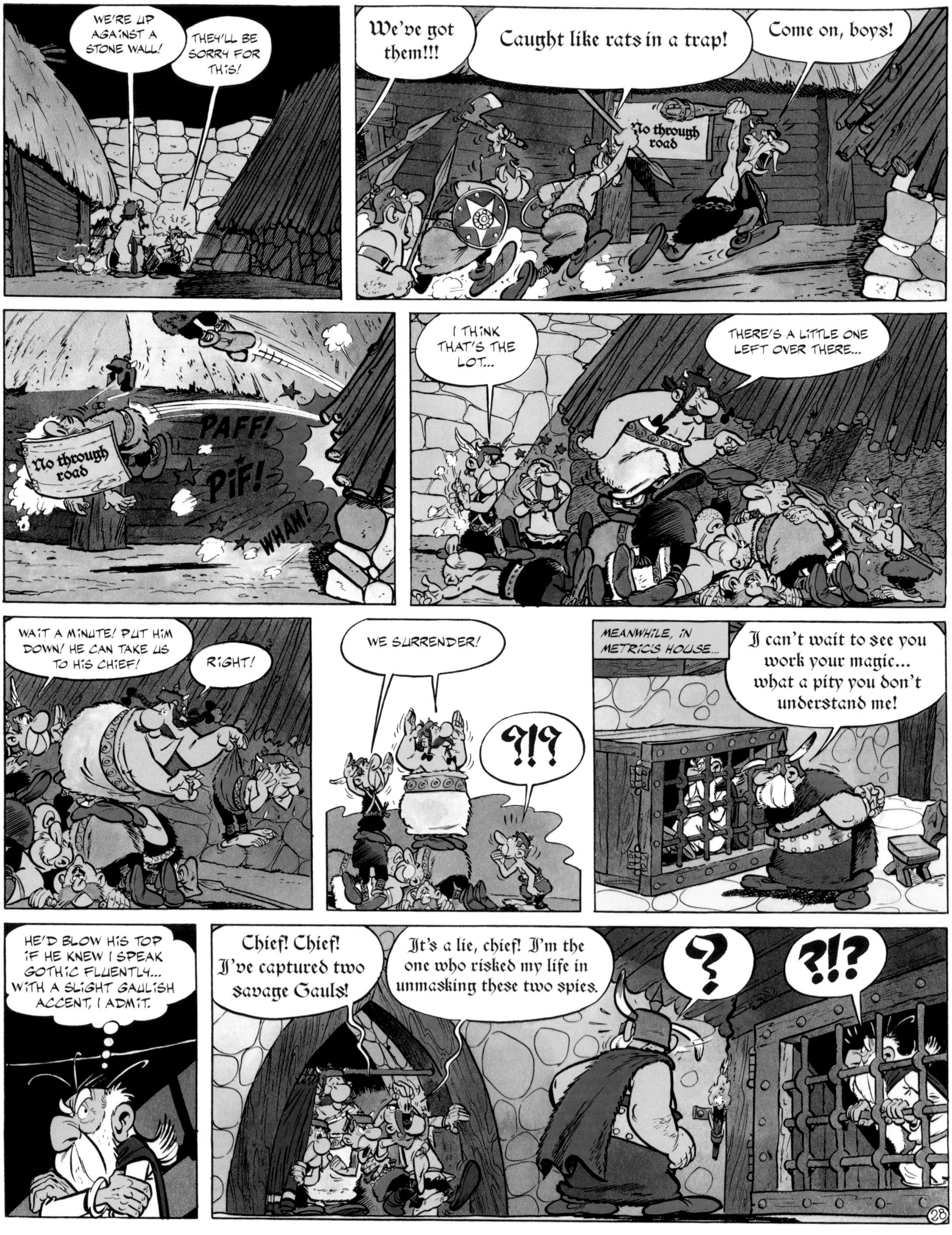
WE'RE UP AGAINST A STONE WALL!
THEY'LL BE SORRY FOR THIS!
We've got them!!!
Caught like rats in a trap!
Come on, boys!
No through road
No through road
PAFF!
PIF!
WHAM!
I THINK THAT'S THE LOT...
THERE'S A LITTLE ONE LEFT OVER THERE...
WAIT A MINUTE! PUT HIM DOWN! HE CAN TAKE US TO HIS CHIEF!
RIGHT!
WE SURRENDER!
?!?
MEANWHILE, IN METRIC'S HOUSE...
I can't wait to see you work your magic... what a pity you don't understand me!
HE'D BLOW HIS TOP IF HE KNEW I SPEAK GOTHIC FLUENTLY... WITH A SLIGHT GAULISH ACCENT, I ADMIT.
Chief! Chief! I've captured two savage Gauls!
It's a lie, chief! I'm the one who risked my life in unmasking these two spies.
?
?!?
28

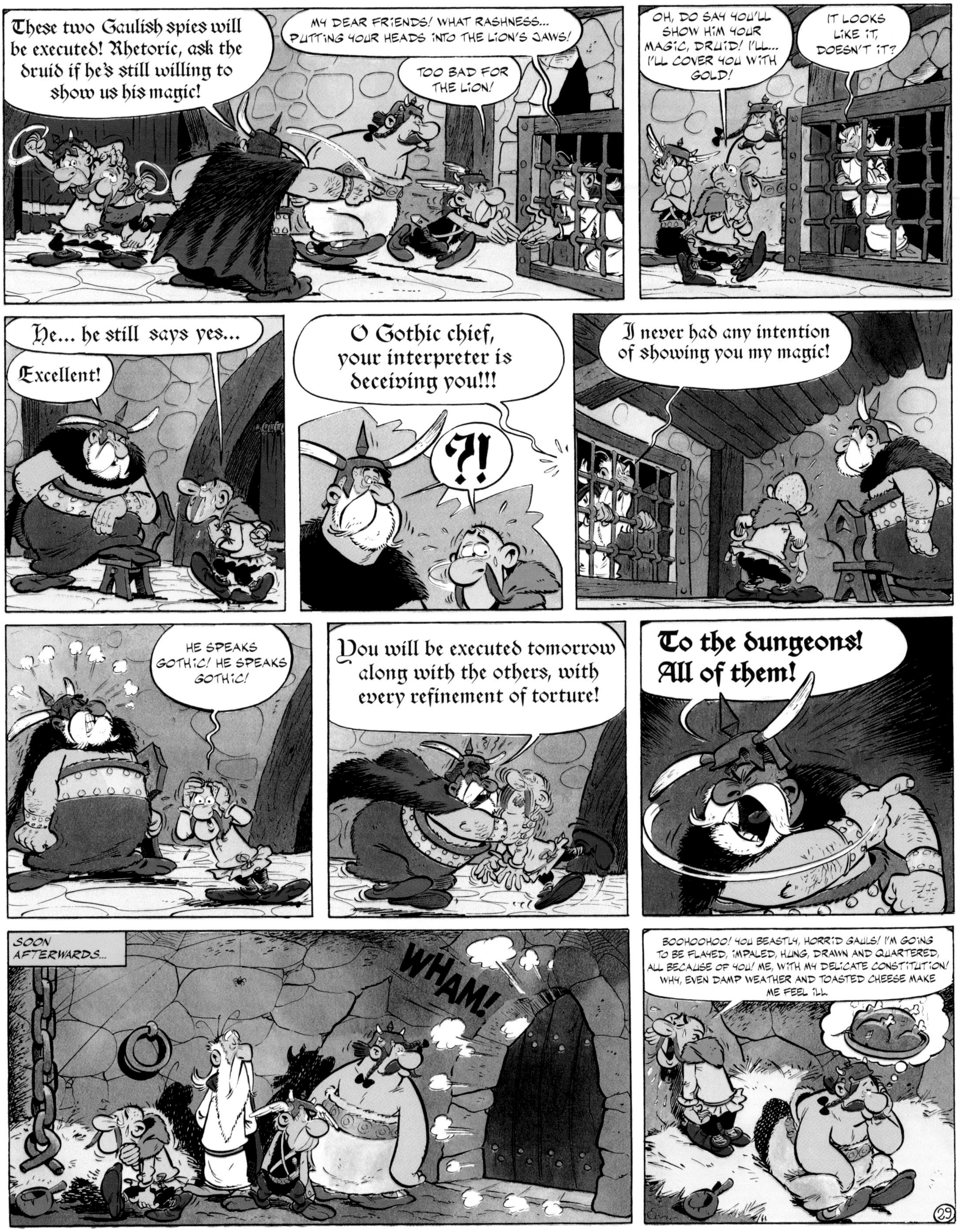
These two Gaulish spies will be executed! Rhetoric, ask the druid if he's still willing to show us his magic!
MY DEAR FRIENDS! WHAT RASHNESS... PUTTING YOUR HEADS INTO THE LION'S JAWS!
TOO BAD FOR THE LION!
OH, DO SAY YOU'LL SHOW HIM YOUR MAGIC, DRUID! I'LL... I'LL COVER YOU WITH GOLD!
IT LOOKS LIKE IT, DOESN'T IT?
He... he still says yes...
Excellent!
O Gothic chief, your interpreter is deceiving you!!!
?!
I never had any intention of showing you my magic!
HE SPEAKS GOTHIC! HE SPEAKS GOTHIC!
You will be executed tomorrow along with the others, with every refinement of torture!
To the dungeons! All of them!
SOON AFTERWARDS...
WHAM!
BOOHOOHOO! YOU BEASTLY, HORRID GAULS! I'M GOING TO BE FLAYED, IMPALED, HUNG, DRAWN AND QUARTERED, ALL BECAUSE OF YOU! ME, WITH MY DELICATE CONSTITUTION! WHY, EVEN DAMP WEATHER AND TOASTED CHEESE MAKE ME FEEL ILL.
29

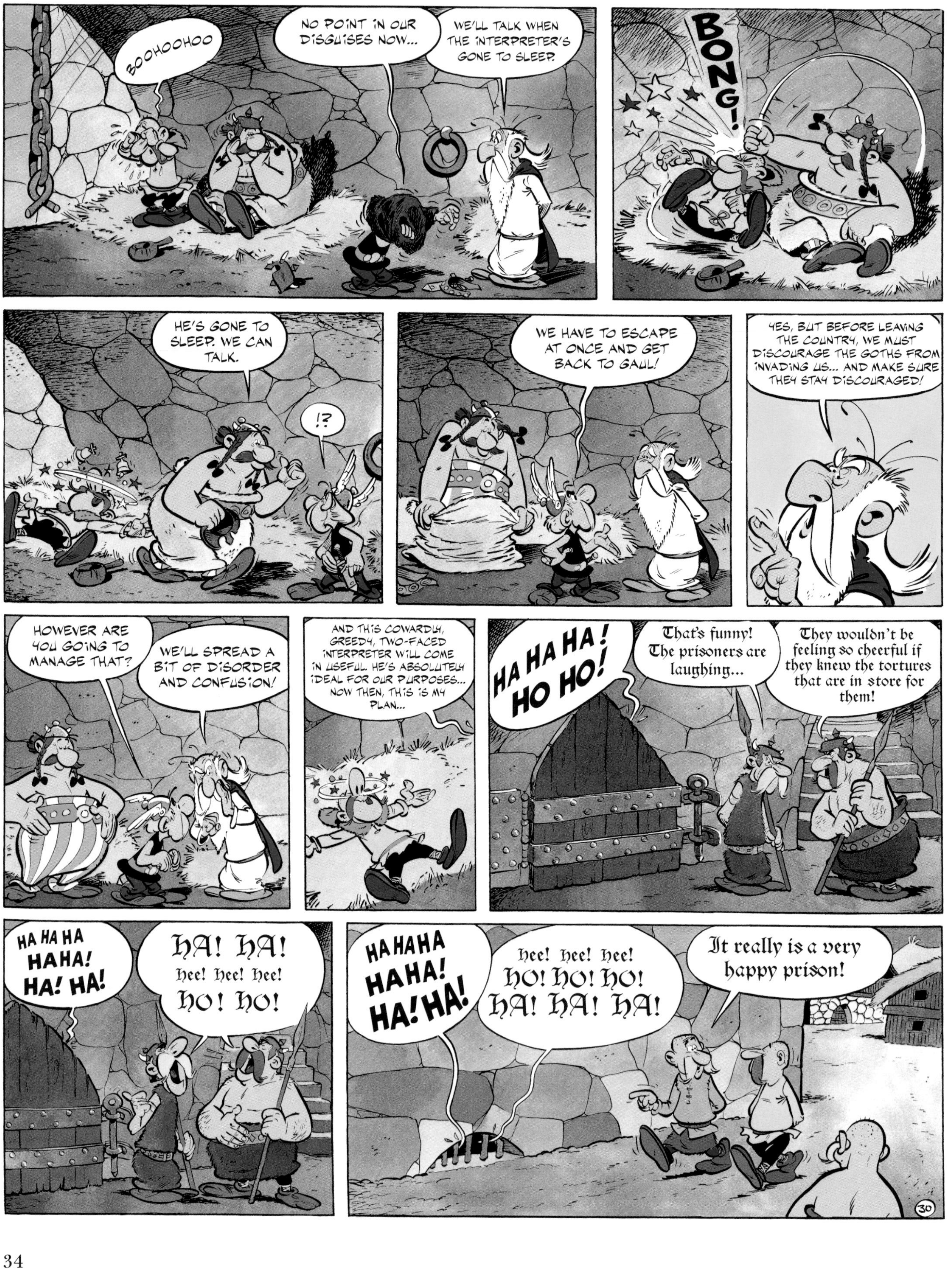
BOOHOOHOO
NO POINT IN OUR DISGUISES NOW...
WE'LL TALK WHEN THE INTERPRETER'S GONE TO SLEEP.
BONG!
HE'S GONE TO SLEEP. WE CAN TALK.
!?
WE HAVE TO ESCAPE AT ONCE AND GET BACK TO GAUL!
YES, BUT BEFORE LEAVING THE COUNTRY, WE MUST DISCOURAGE THE GOTHS FROM INVADING US... AND MAKE SURE THEY STAY DISCOURAGED!
HOWEVER ARE YOU GOING TO MANAGE THAT?
WE'LL SPREAD A BIT OF DISORDER AND CONFUSION!
AND THIS COWARDLY, GREEDY, TWO-FACED INTERPRETER WILL COME IN USEFUL. HE'S ABSOLUTELY IDEAL FOR OUR PURPOSES... NOW THEN, THIS IS MY PLAN...
HA HA HA! HO HO!
That's funny! The prisoners are laughing...
They wouldn't be feeling so cheerful if they knew the tortures that are in store for them!
HA HA HA HAHA! HA! HA!
HA! HA! Hee! Hee! Hee! HO! HO!
HA HA HA HAHA! HA! HA!
Hee! Hee! Hee! HO! HO! HO! HA! HA! HA!
It really is a very happy prison!
30

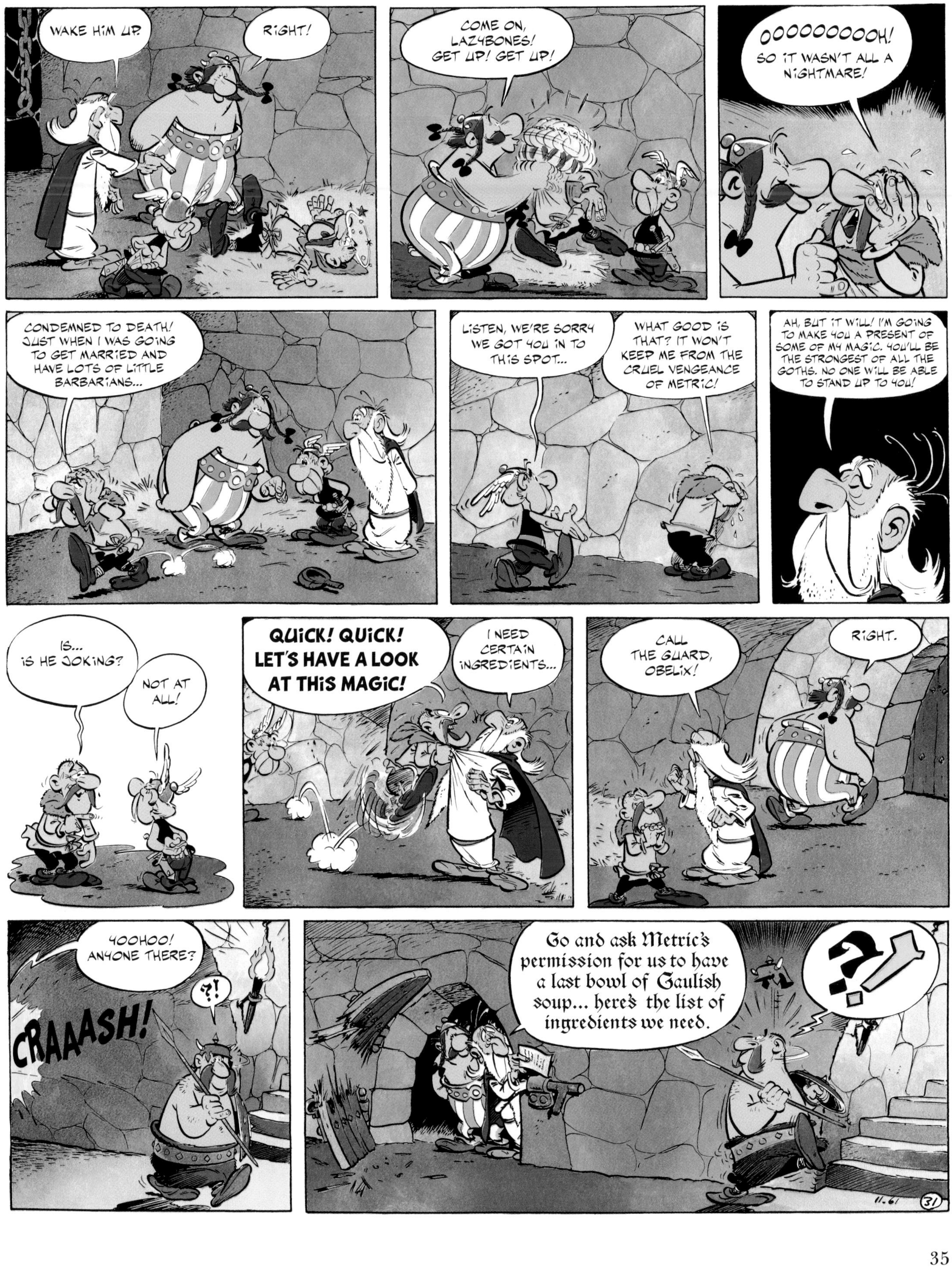
WAKE HIM UP.
RIGHT!
COME ON, LAZYBONES! GET UP! GET UP!
OOOOOOOOOH! SO IT WASN'T ALL A NIGHTMARE!
CONDEMNED TO DEATH! JUST WHEN I WAS GOING TO GET MARRIED AND HAVE LOTS OF LITTLE BARBARIANS...
LISTEN, WE'RE SORRY WE GOT YOU IN TO THIS SPOT...
WHAT GOOD IS THAT? IT WON'T KEEP ME FROM THE CRUEL VENGEANCE OF METRIC!
AH, BUT IT WILL! I'M GOING TO MAKE YOU A PRESENT OF SOME OF MY MAGIC. YOU'LL BE THE STRONGEST OF ALL THE GOTHS. NO ONE WILL BE ABLE TO STAND UP TO YOU!
IS... IS HE JOKING?
NOT AT ALL!
QUICK! QUICK! LET'S HAVE A LOOK AT THIS MAGIC!
I NEED CERTAIN INGREDIENTS...
CALL THE GUARD, OBELIX!
RIGHT.
YOOHOO! ANYONE THERE?
CRAAASH!
?!
Go and ask Metric's permission for us to have a last bowl of Gaulish soup... here's the list of ingredients we need.
?!
11.61
31

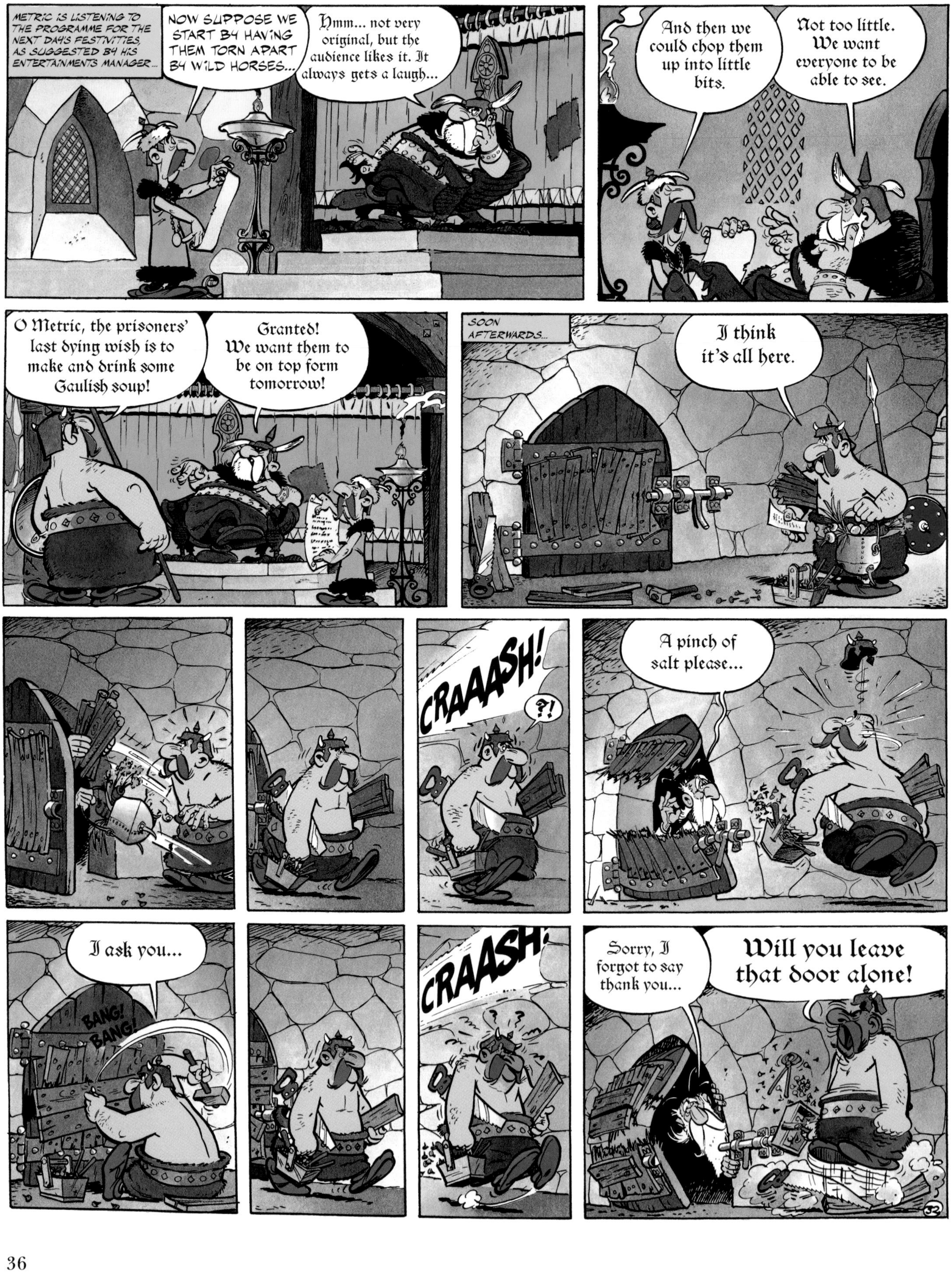
METRIC IS LISTENING TO THE PROGRAMME FOR THE NEXT DAY'S FESTIVITIES, AS SUGGESTED BY HIS ENTERTAINMENTS MANAGER...
NOW SUPPOSE WE START BY HAVING THEM TORN APART BY WILD HORSES...
Hmm... not very original, but the audience likes it. It always gets a laugh...
And then we could chop them up into little bits.
Not too little. We want everyone to be able to see.
O Metric, the prisoners' last dying wish is to make and drink some Gaulish soup!
Granted! We want them to be on top form tomorrow!
SOON AFTERWARDS...
I think it's all here.
CRAAASH!
?!
A pinch of salt please...
I ask you...
BANG! BANG!
CRAAASH!
Sorry, I forgot to say thank you...
Will you leave that door alone!

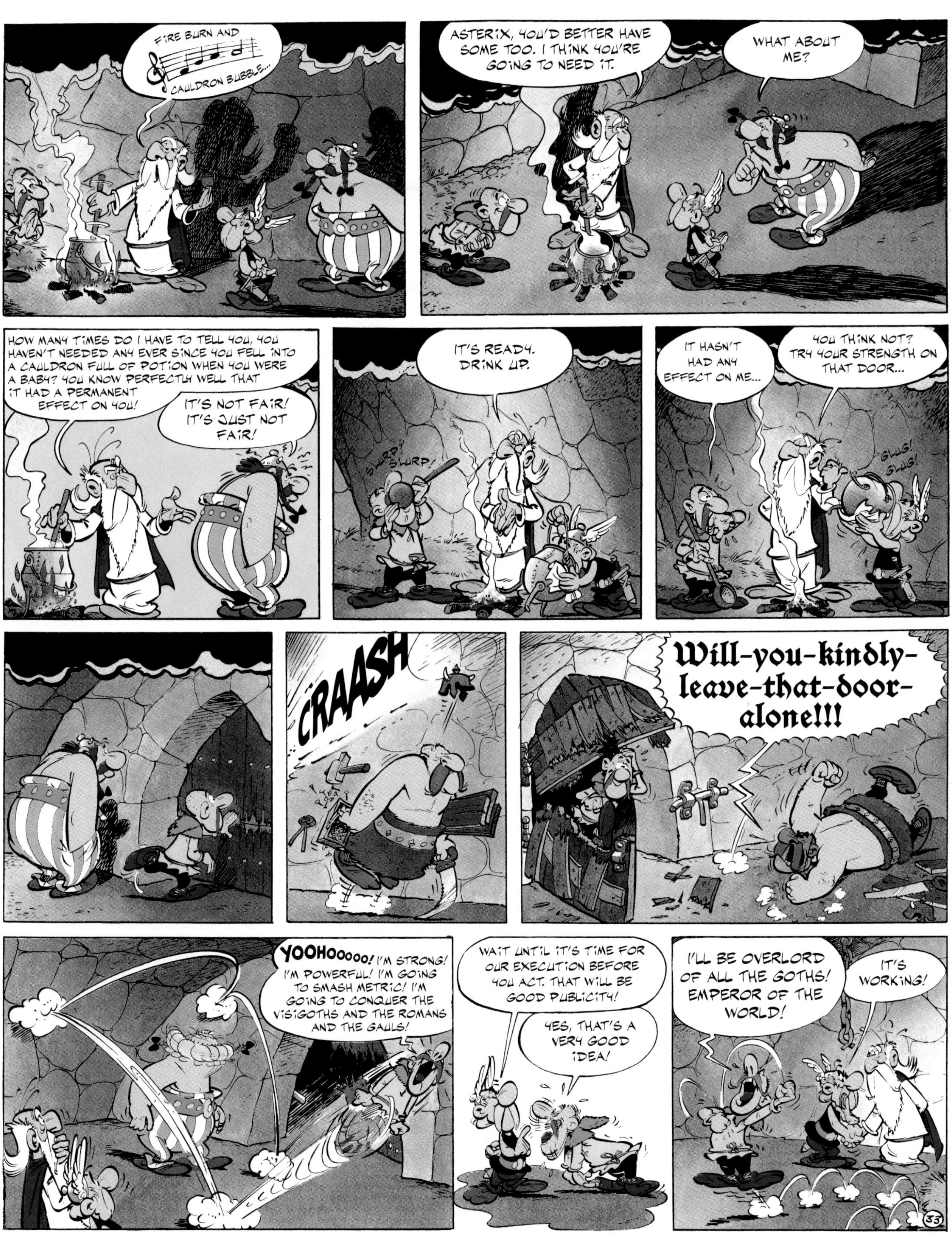
FIRE BURN AND CAULDRON BUBBLE...
ASTERIX, YOU'D BETTER HAVE SOME TOO. I THINK YOU'RE GOING TO NEED IT.
WHAT ABOUT ME?
HOW MANY TIMES DO I HAVE TO TELL YOU, YOU HAVEN'T NEEDED ANY EVER SINCE YOU FELL INTO A CAULDRON FULL OF POTION WHEN YOU WERE A BABY? YOU KNOW PERFECTLY WELL THAT IT HAD A PERMANENT EFFECT ON YOU!
IT'S NOT FAIR! IT'S JUST NOT FAIR!
IT'S READY. DRINK UP.
SLURP! SLURP!
IT HASN'T HAD ANY EFFECT ON ME...
YOU THINK NOT? TRY YOUR STRENGTH ON THAT DOOR...
GLUG! GLUG!
CRAASH
Will-you-kindly-leave-that-door-alone!!!
YOOHOooooo! I'M STRONG! I'M POWERFUL! I'M GOING TO SMASH METRIC! I'M GOING TO CONQUER THE VISIGOTHS AND THE ROMANS AND THE GAULS!
WAIT UNTIL IT'S TIME FOR OUR EXECUTION BEFORE YOU ACT. THAT WILL BE GOOD PUBLICITY!
YES, THAT'S A VERY GOOD IDEA!
I'LL BE OVERLORD OF ALL THE GOTHS! EMPEROR OF THE WORLD!
IT'S WORKING!
33

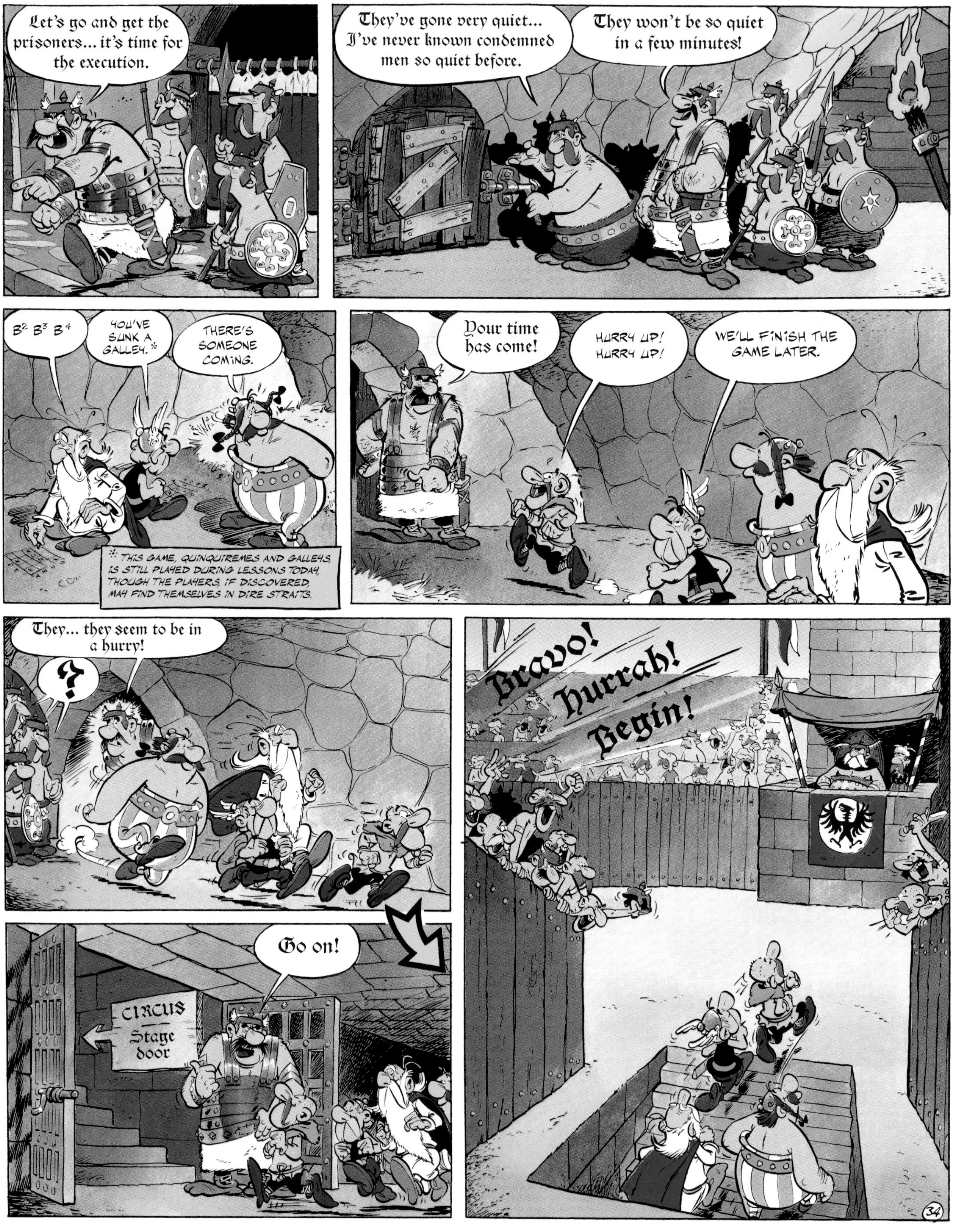

Let's go and get the prisoners... it's time for the execution.
They've gone very quiet... I've never known condemned men so quiet before.
They won't be so quiet in a few minutes!
B2 B3 B4
YOU'VE SUNK A GALLEY.*
THERE'S SOMEONE COMING.
* THIS GAME, QUINQUIREMES AND GALLEYS, IS STILL PLAYED DURING LESSONS TODAY, THOUGH THE PLAYERS, IF DISCOVERED, MAY FIND THEMSELVES IN DIRE STRAITS.
Your time has come!
HURRY UP! HURRY UP!
WE'LL FINISH THE GAME LATER.
They... they seem to be in a hurry!
?
CIRCUS
Stage door
Go on!
Bravo!
Hurrah!
Begin!
34

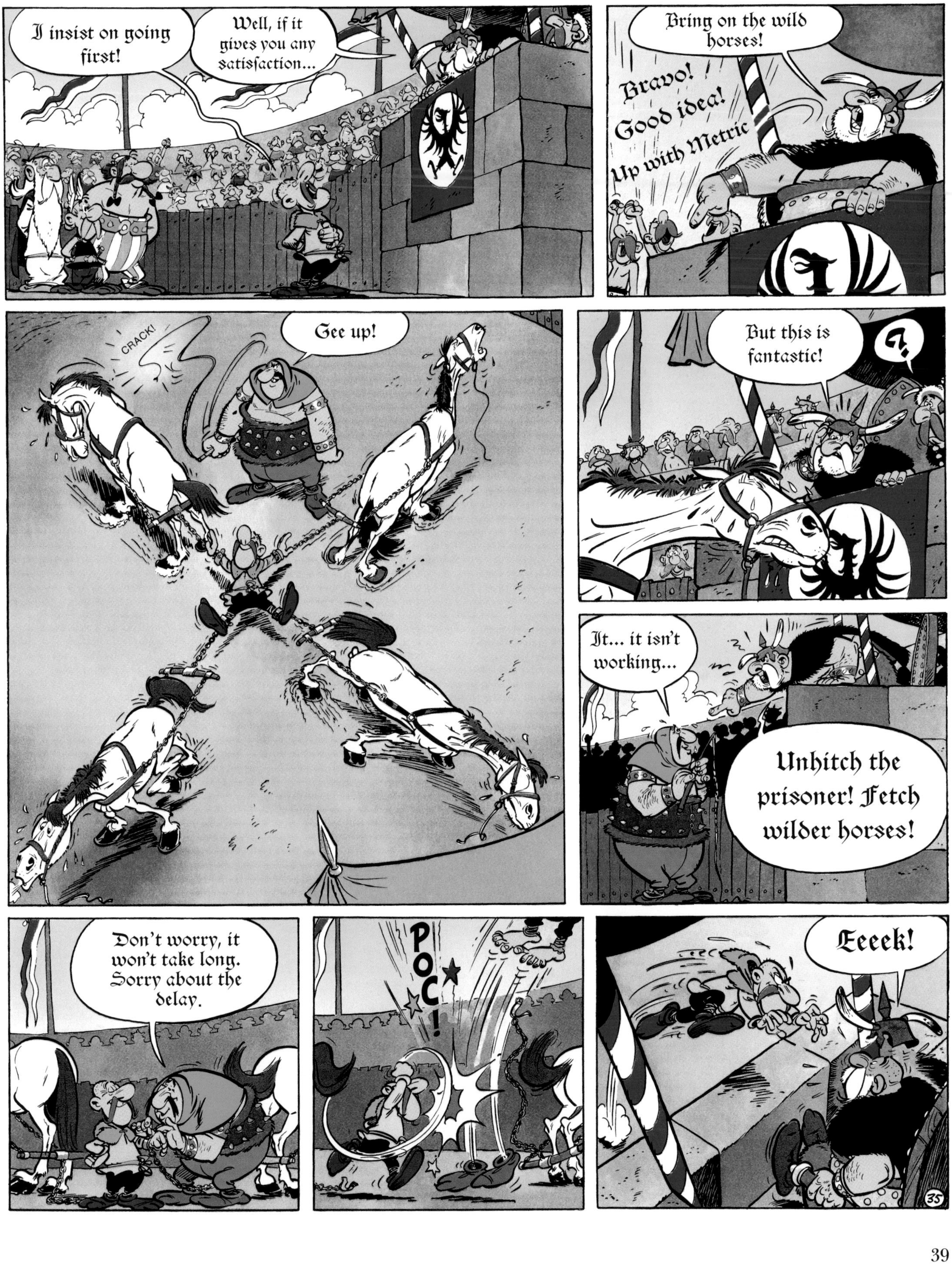
I insist on going first!
Well, if it gives you any satisfaction...
Bring on the wild horses!
Bravo!
Good idea!
Up with Metric
CRACK!
Gee up!
But this is fantastic!
?
It... it isn't working...
Unhitch the prisoner! Fetch wilder horses!
Don't worry, it won't take long. Sorry about the delay.
POC!
Eeeek!
35

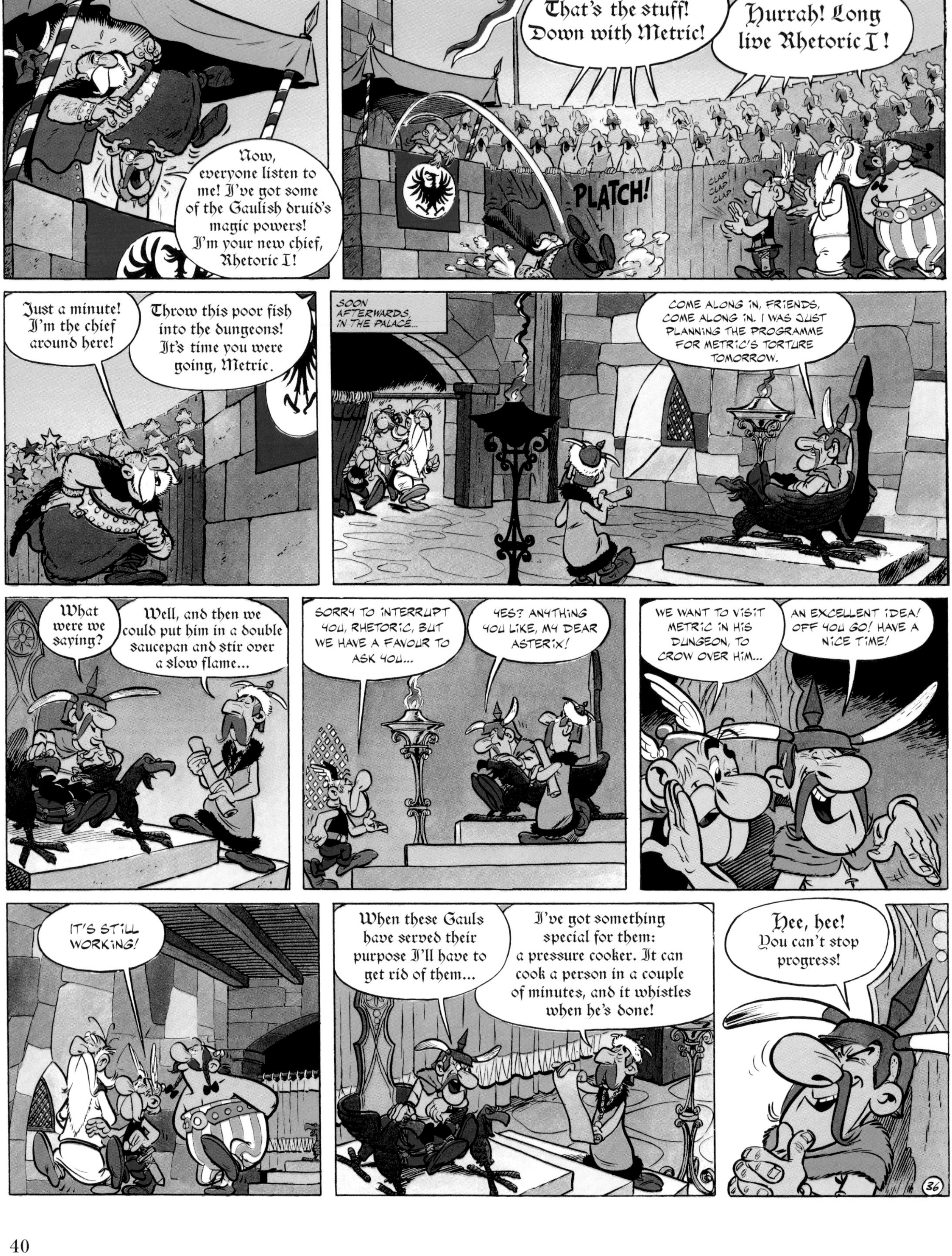
Now, everyone listen to me! I've got some of the Gaulish druid's magic powers! I'm your new chief, Rhetoric I!
That's the stuff! Down with Metric!
Hurrah! Long live Rhetoric I!
PLATCH!
CLAP! CLAP! CLAP!
Just a minute! I'm the chief around here!
Throw this poor fish into the dungeons! It's time you were going, Metric.
SOON AFTERWARDS, IN THE PALACE...
COME ALONG IN, FRIENDS, COME ALONG IN. I WAS JUST PLANNING THE PROGRAMME FOR METRIC'S TORTURE TOMORROW.
What were we saying?
Well, and then we could put him in a double saucepan and stir over a slow flame...
SORRY TO INTERRUPT YOU, RHETORIC, BUT WE HAVE A FAVOUR TO ASK YOU...
YES? ANYTHING YOU LIKE, MY DEAR ASTERIX!
WE WANT TO VISIT METRIC IN HIS DUNGEON, TO CROW OVER HIM...
AN EXCELLENT IDEA! OFF YOU GO! HAVE A NICE TIME!
IT'S STILL WORKING!
When these Gauls have served their purpose I'll have to get rid of them...
I've got something special for them: a pressure cooker. It can cook a person in a couple of minutes, and it whistles when he's done!
Hee, hee! You can't stop progress!
36

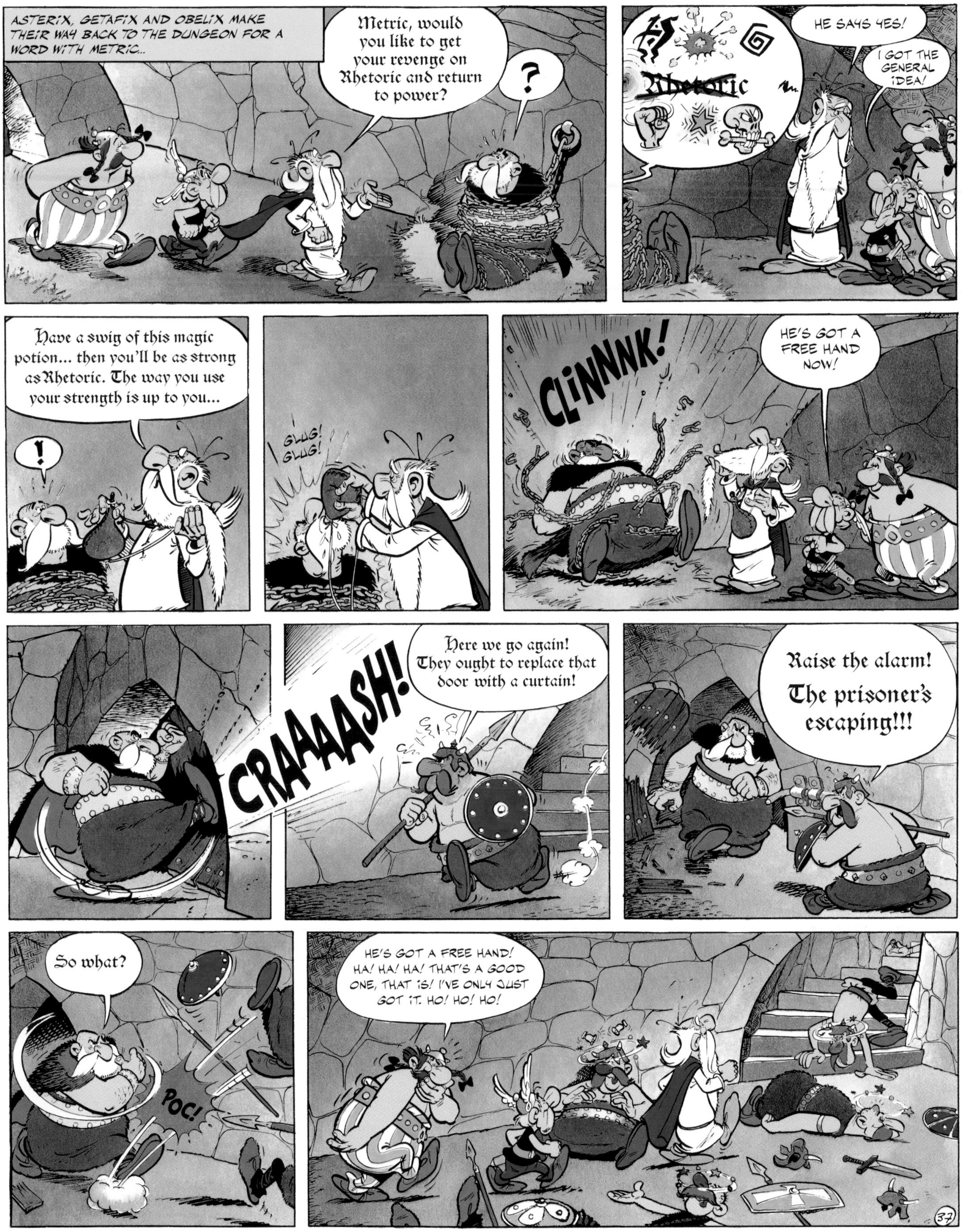

ASTERIX, GETAFIX AND OBELIX MAKE THEIR WAY BACK TO THE DUNGEON FOR A WORD WITH METRIC...
Metric, would you like to get your revenge on Rhetoric and return to power?
?
Rhetoric
HE SAYS YES!
I GOT THE GENERAL IDEA!
Have a swig of this magic potion... then you'll be as strong as Rhetoric. The way you use your strength is up to you...
!
GLUG! GLUG!
CLINNNK!
HE'S GOT A FREE HAND NOW!
CRAAAASH!
Here we go again! They ought to replace that door with a curtain!
Raise the alarm!
The prisoner's escaping!!!
So what?
POC!
HE'S GOT A FREE HAND! HA! HA! HA! THAT'S A GOOD ONE, THAT IS! I'VE ONLY JUST GOT IT. HO! HO! HO!
37

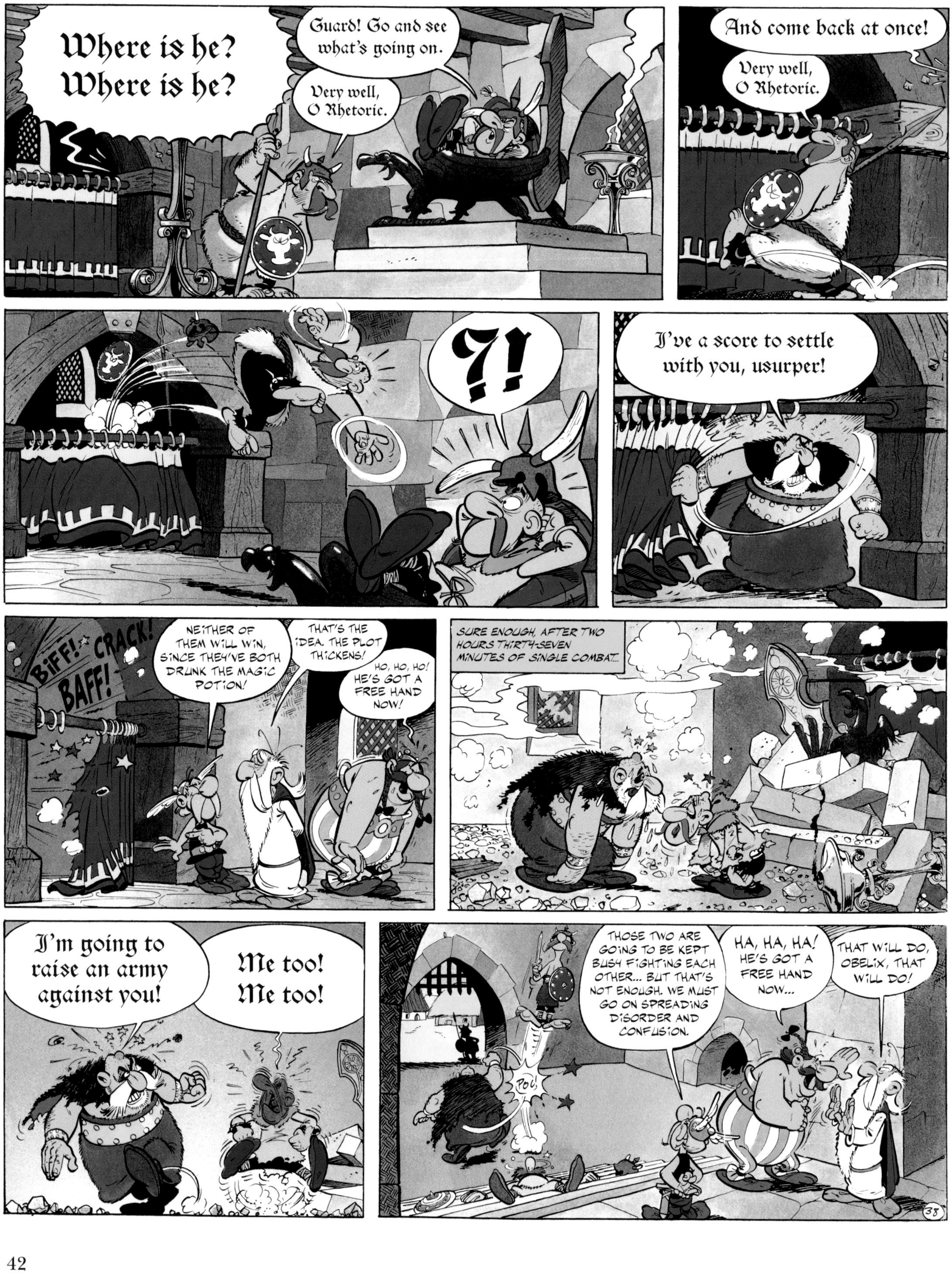
Where is he? Where is he?
Guard! Go and see what's going on.
Very well, O Rhetoric.
And come back at once!
Very well, O Rhetoric.
?!
I've a score to settle with you, usurper!
BIFF! BAFF! CRACK!
NEITHER OF THEM WILL WIN, SINCE THEY'VE BOTH DRUNK THE MAGIC POTION!
THAT'S THE IDEA. THE PLOT THICKENS!
HO, HO, HO! HE'S GOT A FREE HAND NOW!
SURE ENOUGH, AFTER TWO HOURS THIRTY-SEVEN MINUTES OF SINGLE COMBAT...
I'm going to raise an army against you!
Me too! Me too!
POK!
THOSE TWO ARE GOING TO BE KEPT BUSY FIGHTING EACH OTHER... BUT THAT'S NOT ENOUGH. WE MUST GO ON SPREADING DISORDER AND CONFUSION.
HA, HA, HA! HE'S GOT A FREE HAND NOW...
THAT WILL DO, OBELIX, THAT WILL DO!
38

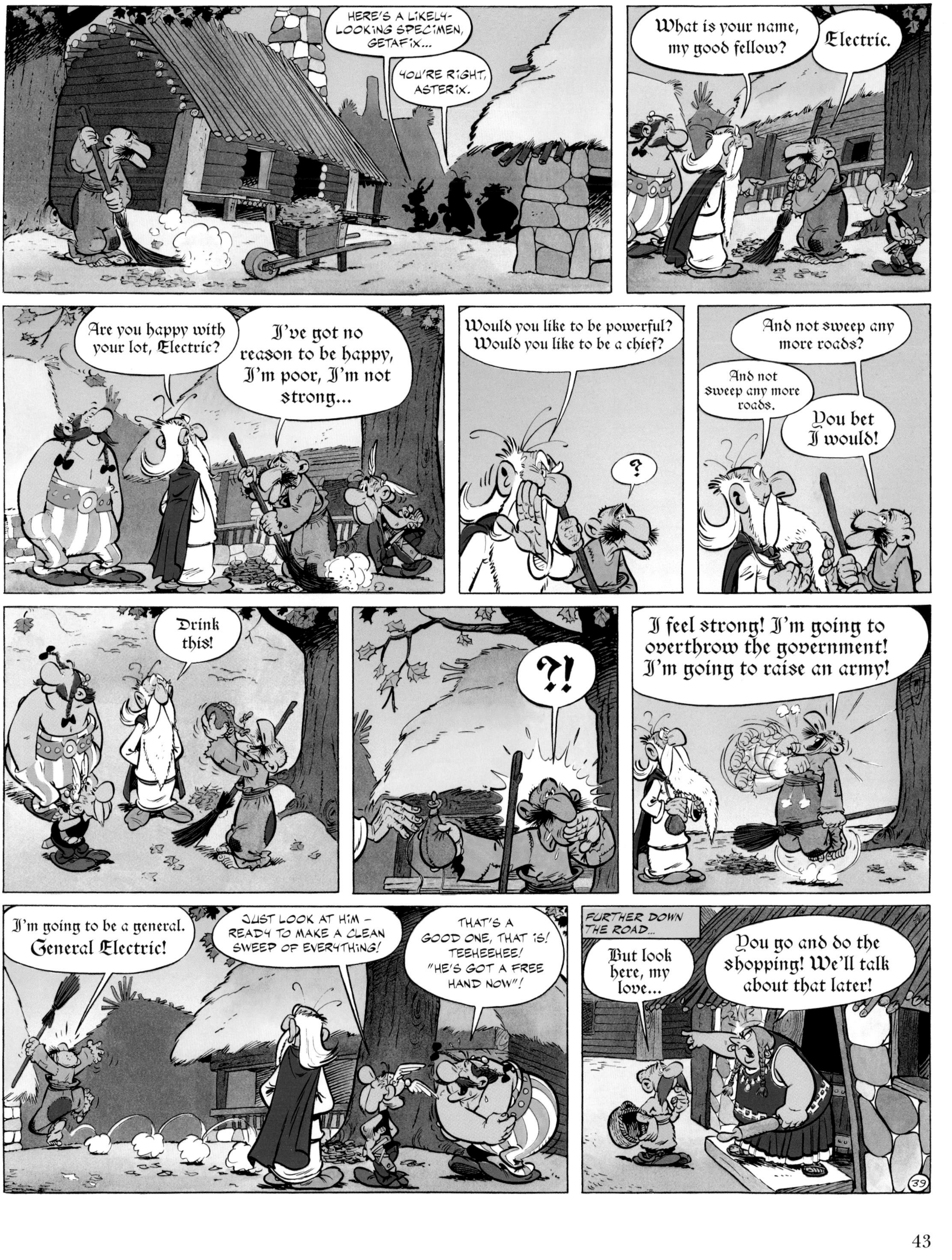
HERE'S A LIKELY-LOOKING SPECIMEN, GETAFIX...
YOU'RE RIGHT, ASTERIX.
What is your name, my good fellow?
Electric.
Are you happy with your lot, Electric?
I've got no reason to be happy, I'm poor, I'm not strong...
Would you like to be powerful? Would you like to be a chief?
?
And not sweep any more roads?
And not sweep any more roads.
You bet I would!
Drink this!
?!
I feel strong! I'm going to overthrow the government! I'm going to raise an army!
I'm going to be a general. General Electric!
JUST LOOK AT HIM – READY TO MAKE A CLEAN SWEEP OF EVERYTHING!
THAT'S A GOOD ONE, THAT IS! TEEHEEHEE! "HE'S GOT A FREE HAND NOW"!
FURTHER DOWN THE ROAD...
But look here, my love...
You go and do the shopping! We'll talk about that later!
39

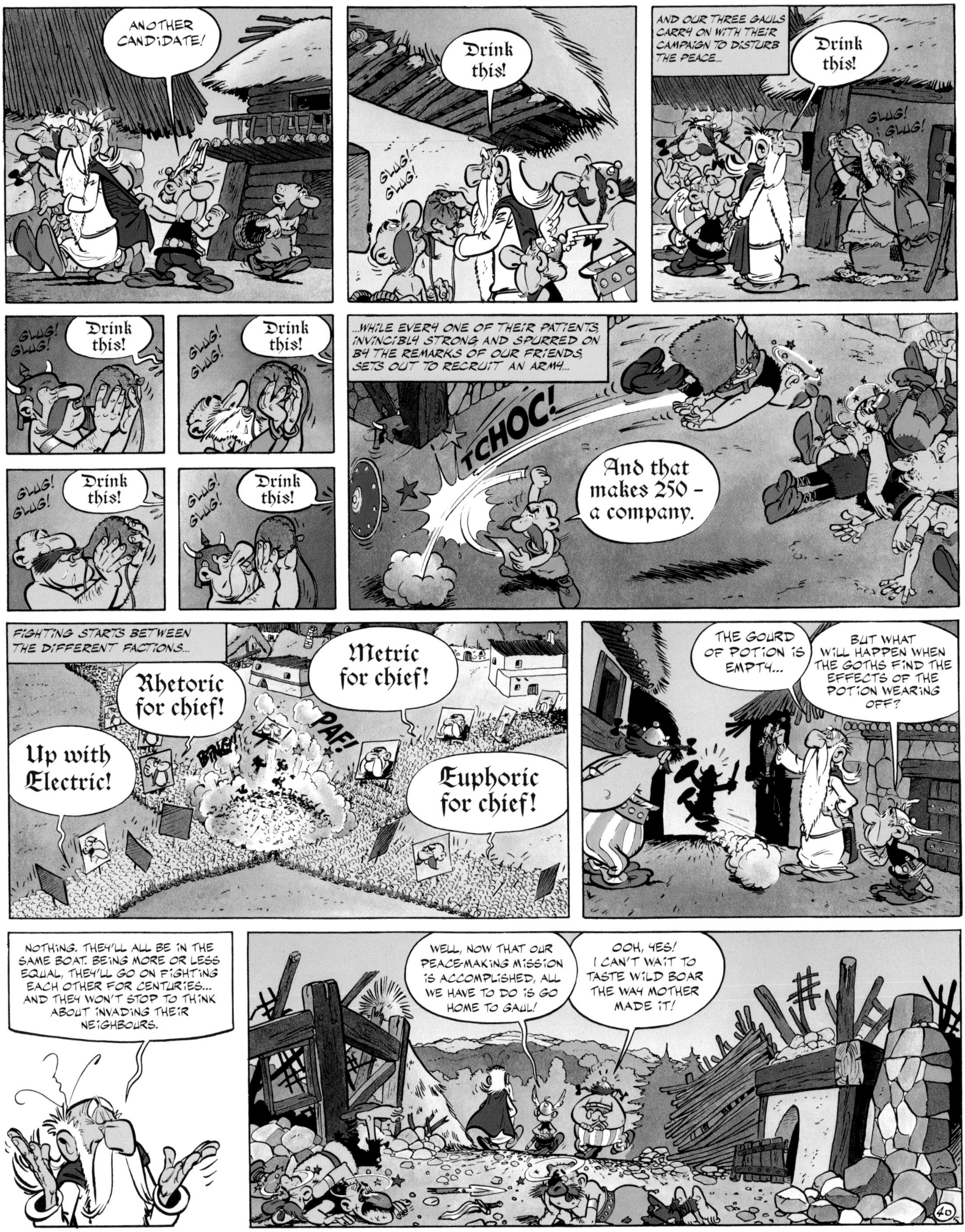

ANOTHER CANDIDATE!
Drink this!
GLUG! GLUG!
AND OUR THREE GAULS CARRY ON WITH THEIR CAMPAIGN TO DISTURB THE PEACE...
Drink this!
GLUG! GLUG!
GLUG! GLUG!
Drink this!
GLUG! GLUG!
Drink this!
GLUG! GLUG!
Drink this!
GLUG! GLUG!
Drink this!
...WHILE EVERY ONE OF THEIR PATIENTS, INVINCIBLY STRONG AND SPURRED ON BY THE REMARKS OF OUR FRIENDS, SETS OUT TO RECRUIT AN ARMY...
TCHOC!
And that makes 250 – a company.
FIGHTING STARTS BETWEEN THE DIFFERENT FACTIONS...
Rhetoric for chief!
Metric for chief!
Up with Electric!
PAF!
BING!
Euphoric for chief!
THE GOURD OF POTION IS EMPTY...
BUT WHAT WILL HAPPEN WHEN THE GOTHS FIND THE EFFECTS OF THE POTION WEARING OFF?
NOTHING. THEY'LL ALL BE IN THE SAME BOAT. BEING MORE OR LESS EQUAL, THEY'LL GO ON FIGHTING EACH OTHER FOR CENTURIES... AND THEY WON'T STOP TO THINK ABOUT INVADING THEIR NEIGHBOURS.
WELL, NOW THAT OUR PEACE-MAKING MISSION IS ACCOMPLISHED, ALL WE HAVE TO DO IS GO HOME TO GAUL!
OOH, YES! I CAN'T WAIT TO TASTE WILD BOAR THE WAY MOTHER MADE IT!
40

SOME OF THE CHIEFS

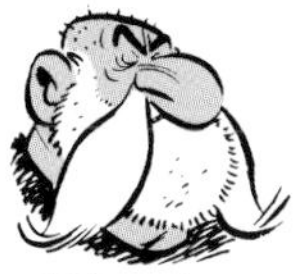

Metric

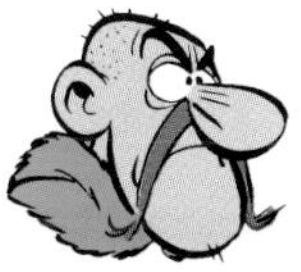

Rhetoric

THE ASTERIXIAN WARS

A Tangled Web...

The ruse employed by Asterix, Getafix and Obelix succeeded beyond their wildest dreams. After drinking the druid's magic potion, the Goths fought each other tooth and nail. Here is a brief summary to help you follow the history of these famous wars.

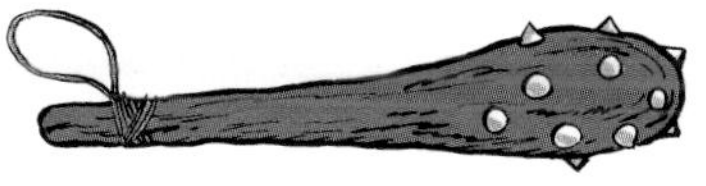

The favourite and devastating weapon of the combatants.

Diagram indicating the course of events.

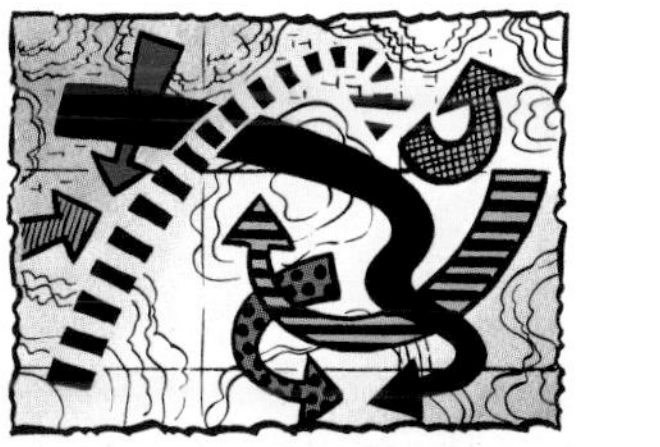

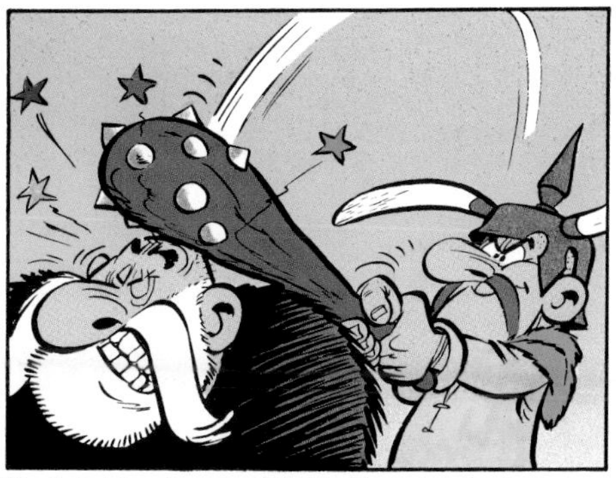

The first victory is won outright by Rhetoric, who, having surprised Metric by an outflanking movement, lets him have it – bonk! – and inflicts a crushing defeat on him. This defeat, however, is only temporary...

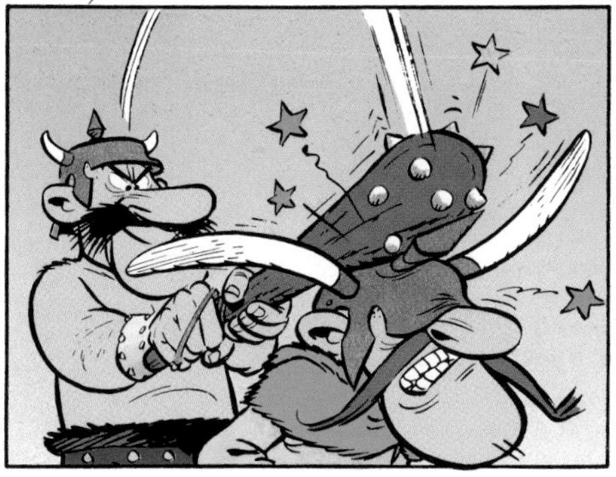

Rhetoric has no time to celebrate his victory, for, having completed his outflanking movement, he is taken in the rear by his own ally, Lyric. Lyric instantly proclaims himself supreme chief of all the Goths, much to the amusement of the other chiefs...

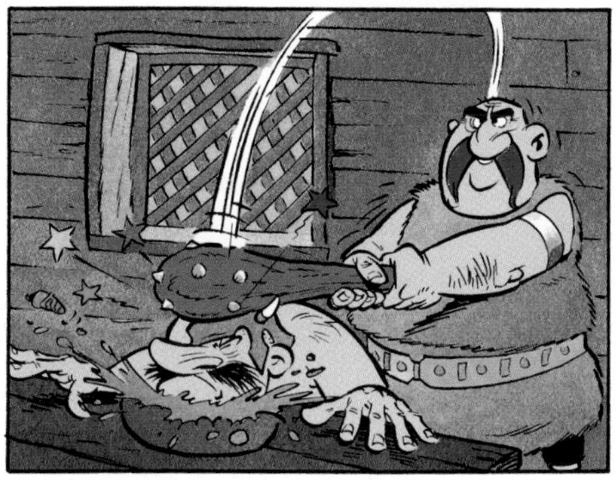

Who turn out to be right, for Lyric's brother-in-law Satiric lays an ambush for him, pretending to invite him to a family reunion, and Lyric falls into the trap. It was upon this occasion that the proposition that blood is thicker than water was first put to the test...

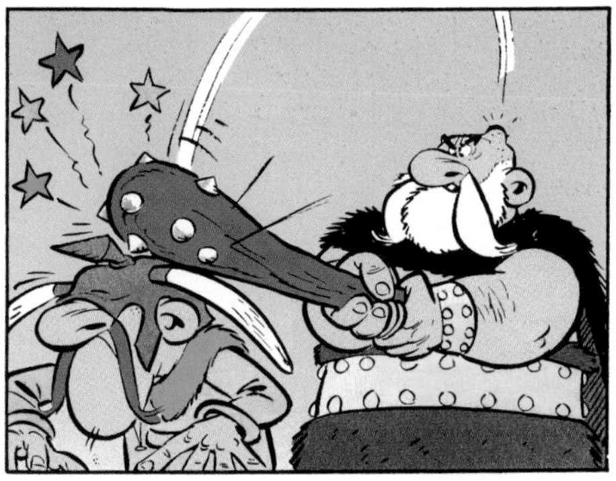

Rhetoric goes after Lyric, with the avowed intention of "bashing him up" (archaic), but his rearguard is surprised by Metric's vanguard. Bonk! This manoeuvre is known as the Metric System.

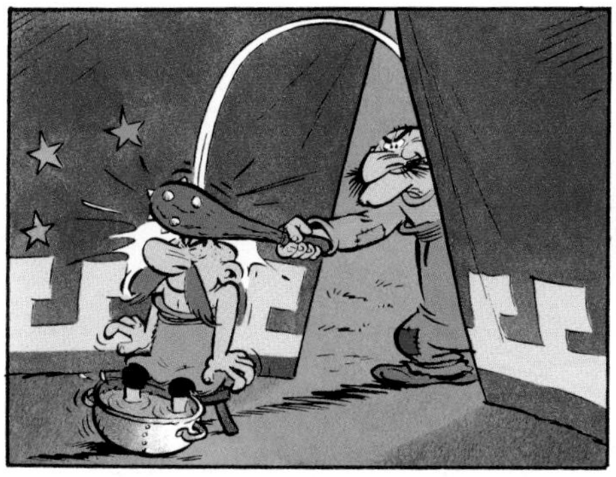

General Electric manages to surprise Euphoric meditating on the conduct of his next few campaigns. Euphoric's morale is distinctly lowered, but he has the last word, with his famous remark, "I'll short-circuit him yet".

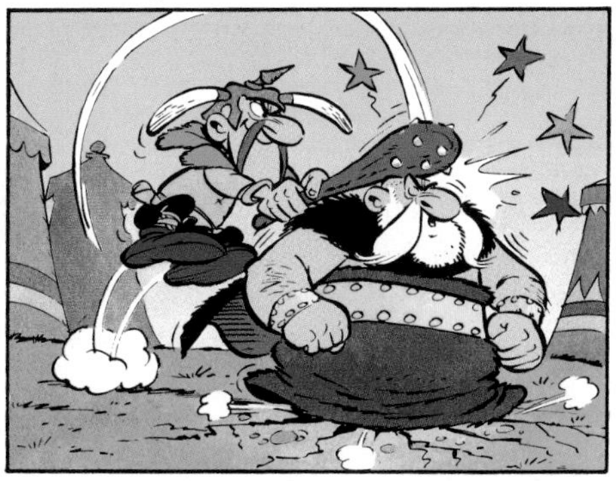

While Electric proclaims himself supreme chief of the Goths, to the amusement of all and sundry, it is the turn of Metric's rearguard to be surprised by Rhetoric's vanguard. Bonk! "This is bad for my system," is the comment of the exasperated Metric.

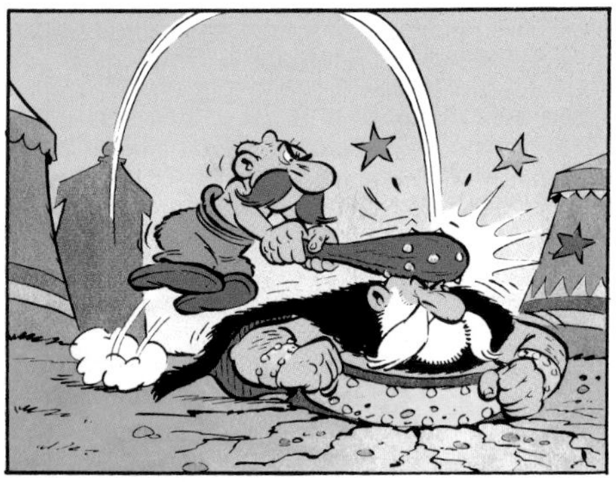

In fact, it is so bad for his system that he allows himself to be surprised by Euphoric. The battle is short and sharp. Euphoric, a wily politician, instantly proclaims himself supreme chief of the Goths. The other supreme chiefs are in fits...

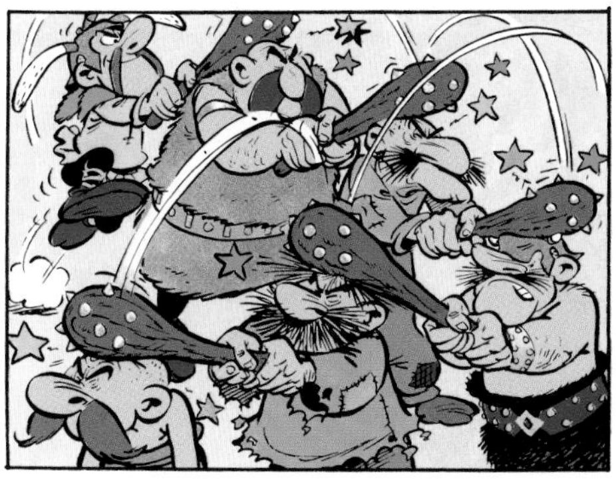

Euphoric, much annoyed, sets up camp and decides to sulk. He is surprised by Eccentric, who in his turn is attacked by Lyric, subsequently to be defeated by Electric. Electric is destined to be betrayed by Satiric, who will be beaten by Rhetoric.

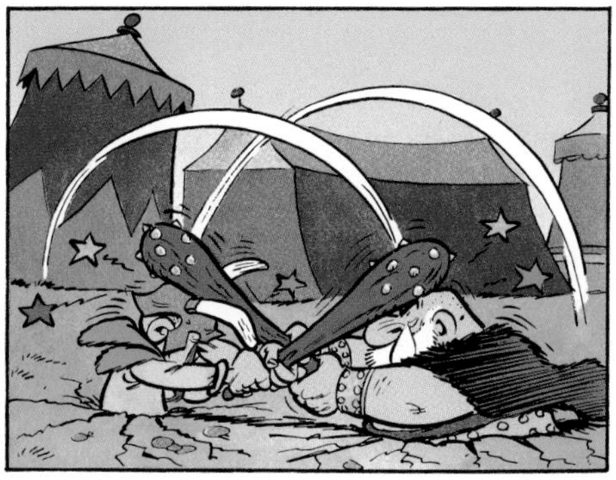

Going round a corner, Rhetoric's vanguard bumps into Metric's vanguard. Bonk! Bonk! This battle is famous in the Asterixian wars as the "Battle of the Two Losers". And so the war goes on...

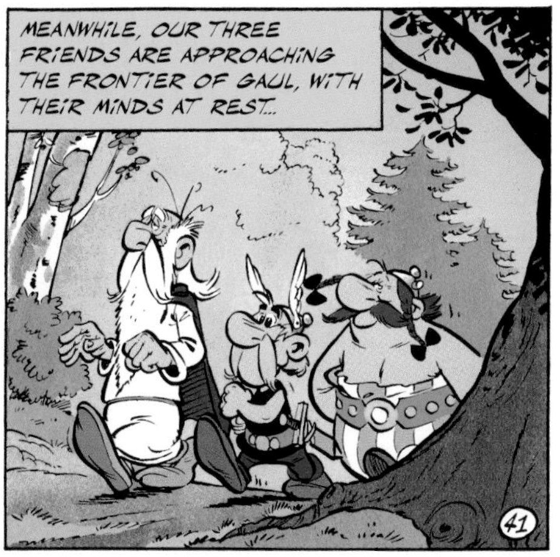
MEANWHILE, OUR THREE FRIENDS ARE APPROACHING THE FRONTIER OF GAUL, WITH THEIR MINDS AT REST...
41

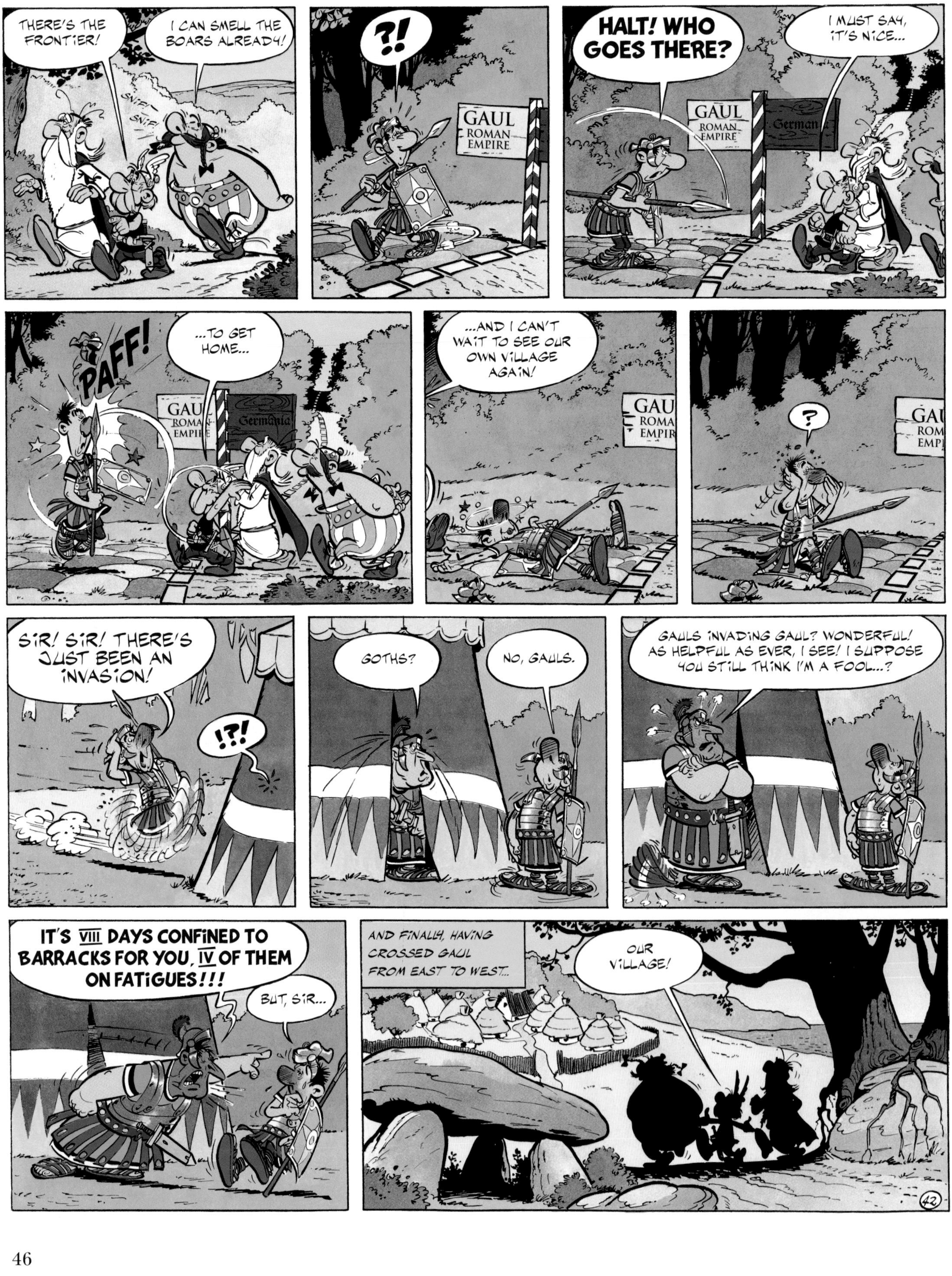

THERE'S THE FRONTIER!
I CAN SMELL THE BOARS ALREADY!
SNIF! SNIF!
?!
GAUL ROMAN EMPIRE
HALT! WHO GOES THERE?
I MUST SAY, IT'S NICE...
GAUL ROMAN EMPIRE
Germania
PAFF!
...TO GET HOME...
GAUL ROMAN EMPIRE
Germania
...AND I CAN'T WAIT TO SEE OUR OWN VILLAGE AGAIN!
?
SIR! SIR! THERE'S JUST BEEN AN INVASION!
!?!
GOTHS?
NO, GAULS.
GAULS INVADING GAUL? WONDERFUL! AS HELPFUL AS EVER, I SEE! I SUPPOSE YOU STILL THINK I'M A FOOL...?
IT'S VIII DAYS CONFINED TO BARRACKS FOR YOU, IV OF THEM ON FATIGUES!!!
BUT, SIR...
AND FINALLY, HAVING CROSSED GAUL FROM EAST TO WEST...
OUR VILLAGE!
42

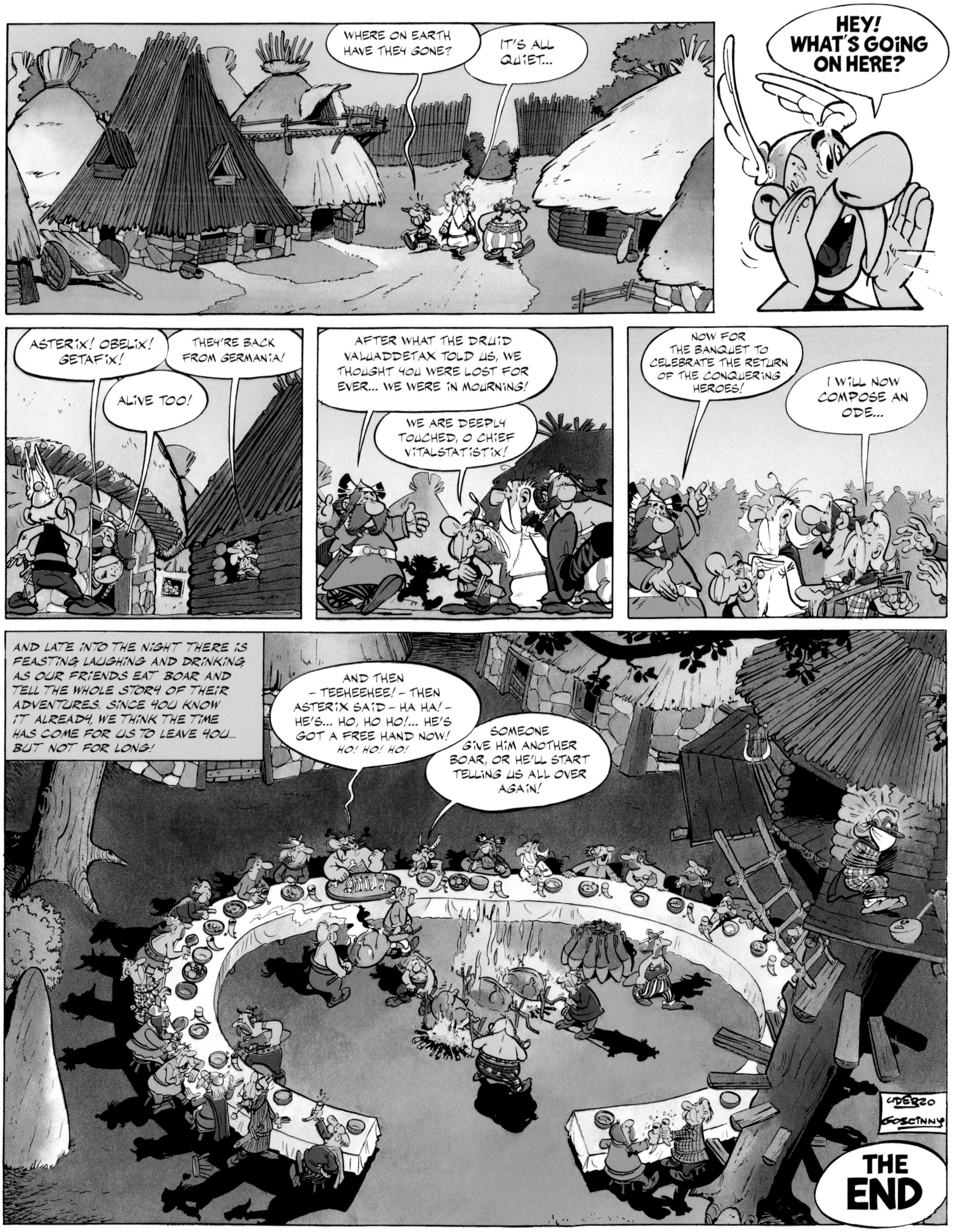
WHERE ON EARTH HAVE THEY GONE?
IT'S ALL QUIET...
HEY! WHAT'S GOING ON HERE?
ASTERIX! OBELIX! GETAFIX!
THEY'RE BACK FROM GERMANIA!
ALIVE TOO!
AFTER WHAT THE DRUID VALUADDETAX TOLD US, WE THOUGHT YOU WERE LOST FOR EVER... WE WERE IN MOURNING!
WE ARE DEEPLY TOUCHED, O CHIEF VITALSTATISTIX!
NOW FOR THE BANQUET TO CELEBRATE THE RETURN OF THE CONQUERING HEROES!
I WILL NOW COMPOSE AN ODE...
AND LATE INTO THE NIGHT THERE IS FEASTING LAUGHING AND DRINKING AS OUR FRIENDS EAT BOAR AND TELL THE WHOLE STORY OF THEIR ADVENTURES. SINCE YOU KNOW IT ALREADY, WE THINK THE TIME HAS COME FOR US TO LEAVE YOU... BUT NOT FOR LONG!
AND THEN – TEEHEEHEE! – THEN ASTERIX SAID – HA HA! – HE'S... HO, HO HO!... HE'S GOT A FREE HAND NOW! HO! HO! HO!
SOMEONE GIVE HIM ANOTHER BOAR, OR HE'LL START TELLING US ALL OVER AGAIN!
UDERZO
GOSCINNY
THE END

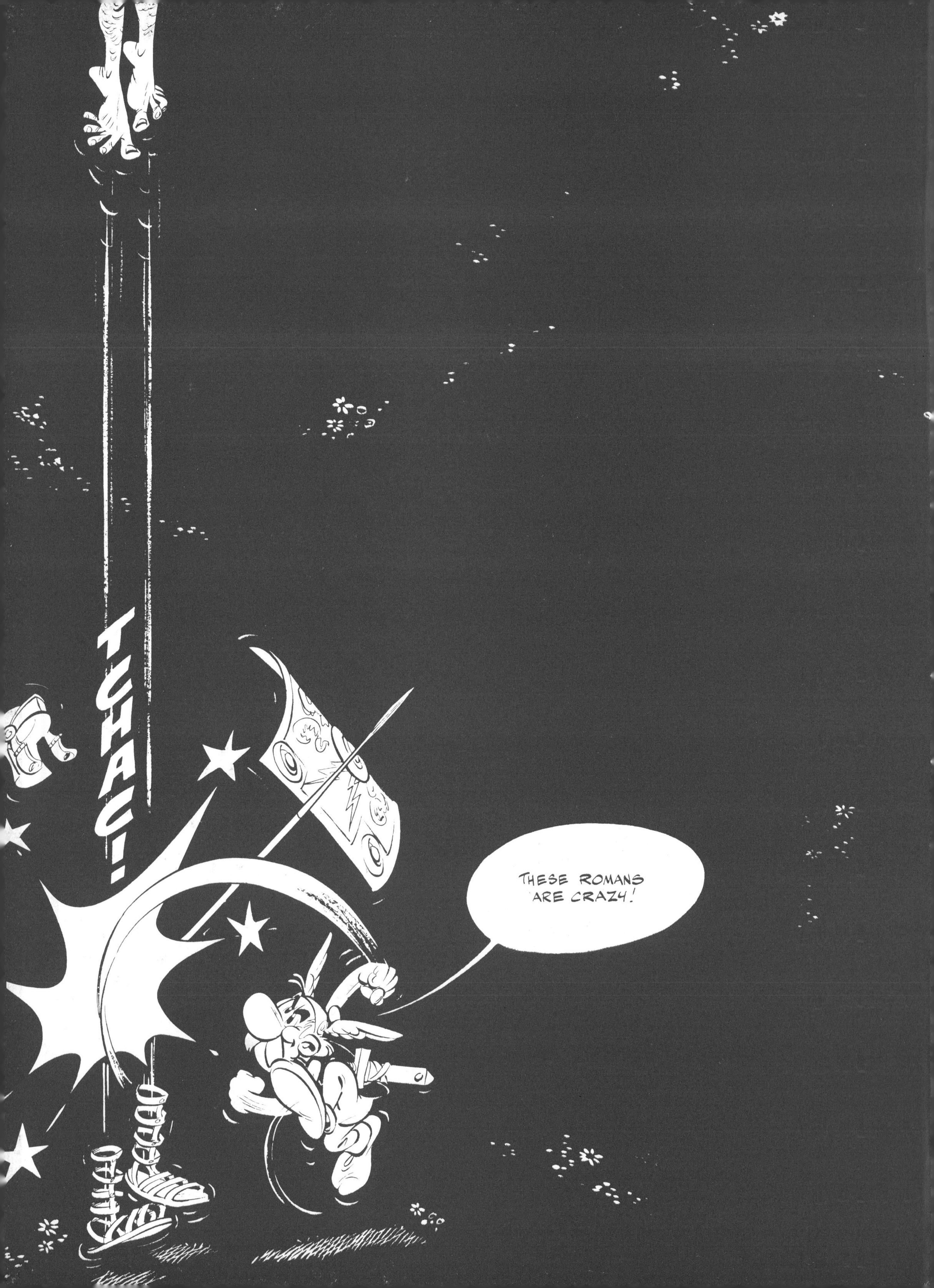
TCHAC!
THESE ROMANS ARE CRAZY!